Lord of
Vice

ERICA RIDLEY

ISBN: 1943794138
ISBN-13: 978-1943794133

This is a work of fiction. Names, characters, places, and in-
cidents are the product of the author's imagination or are
used fictitiously. Any resemblance to actual events, locales,
or persons, living or dead, is purely coincidental.

Cover design © Erica Ridley.
Photograph © Period Images

Chapter 1

London, 1817

*M*iss Bryony Grenville was seated on the floor polishing a worn pair of lad's boots when the door to her private drawing room flew open.

In a flash, she hid the boots and the polish behind her back—then scowled up at her grinning elder brother.

"Heath, you beast." She placed the boots back before her. "I thought you were Mother, here to scold me anew."

"Has she been in here?" Heath looked about in obvious surprise.

The drawing room had once been the private domain of all four Grenville siblings. Bryony was the only unmarried one left.

"She scolds me everywhere, these days. I'm her pet project." She brightened. "Have you brought me more castoffs to wear?"

"I've brought you something better." He flopped bonelessly onto the overstuffed settee just as he had always done. "First, tell me about Mother. Is she hounding you about marriage again?"

"There's no one else left to hound," she replied morosely. "I'm considering pursuing a career as a violinist just to make myself unmarriageable to Society gentlemen."

Heath grinned. "I've no doubt you could do it."

Bryony perked up. "Really?"

"Not that I recommend such an action," he amended. "While you are indeed the most talented violinist ever to grace London with your music, I seem to recall the tiny detail of you actually hating the instrument."

"I don't hate the violin," she protested. "I don't mind playing in our family musicales. And I willingly volunteer my time at Dahlia's school with a minimal quantity of pouting."

"Because you love your family and enjoy helping other people," Heath pointed out. "But if it's not your passion, trading some boring marriage for a grueling soloist career is exchanging one unhappy circumstance for another. Are you certain there are no suitable gentlemen on the horizon? Even a semi-suitable one that you like marginally better than the violin?"

"None I would make a good match with," she admitted. "I wish there was a way I wouldn't have to marry anyone at all."

"Isn't there?" Heath frowned. "I thought that was what all your investments were for. To become a woman of independent financial means."

She winced. "I gave everything I could to Dahlia's school."

"So did I," he said with a crooked grin. "Yet I find myself here on behalf of one of your investments, so I know you have at least one iron in the fire."

Over the past two years, Bryony had sold all the unencumbered assets she'd earned from what felt like a lifetime of investing in order to make her anonymous donations to her sister's struggling school. All she had left was ownership of one outstanding investment contract and a single property deed.

Those pseudonymous investments had been the one thing giving her hope. Until now.

"It doesn't matter. Mother and Father are determined to wash their hands of me before the end of the Season. He'll marry me off before allowing me financial independence." The unfairness of it made the backs of her eyes prick. "They've given me the same ultimatum they gave Camellia. I've one month to nab an eligible bachelor, or they'll select one for me."

He flinched. "The suitor they selected for Camellia was certainly not her best match."

"They're not hoping for a *personality* match," Bryony reminded him. "According to Mother, as the daughter of a baron I am all but contractually required to wed a man with an even loftier title."

"I can imagine how well that's going," Heath said wryly.

"Dreadful," Bryony said with feeling. "I don't want some gentleman twice my age who will take over my investments and my life and my—"

"What *do* you want?" he interrupted, laughing. "To take over *his* investments and his life and his—"

"Oh, you." She tossed a pillow at his head. "I don't want to run anyone's life but my own. Yet even that is impossible. Mother is trying her best to curtail my ways. Take up embroidery or somesuch. She says hoydens are 'mannish' and will never attract a good title."

The corners of Heath's mouth twitched. "Lad's clothing is, by definition, *mannish*."

"She doesn't know I sneak out in them," Bryony pointed out.

He tilted his head. "She is right that you won't catch a man that way."

"Why do I have to have one at all?" Bryony asked. "Why can't I just be independent? I want to decide things for *me*, Bryony Grenville. Not from the shadows. Not under a pseudonym. As *myself*."

Heath's gaze filled with sympathy. "If it were up to me..."

Bryony had hoped to remain a spinster of independent means to avoid losing possession of her hard-won assets. Unfortunately, her parents had grander plans.

"I know," she said dejectedly. "Father has put Mother in charge of finding me a husband. She won't rest until I'm under someone's thumb."

"But until then..." He swung himself upright on the settee. "Perhaps I come bearing good news. I'm to report that Max has doubled his offer."

"Doubled?" That changed everything. Bryony hugged herself as she considered this new development.

Max was Maxwell Gideon, owner of the most infamous gambling den in all of London. Not only was his gaming hell named the Cloven Hoof, the scandal columns intimated the owner might be the devil himself. He was rumored to be tall, dark, and sinfully handsome. Rumor had it, the man had the power to steal souls and grant miracles.

Of course, few if any of the gossipy matrons had ever laid eyes on him.

He had no Almack's voucher. No membership to high-in-the-instep gentlemen's clubs like White's or

Brooks's or even the slightly less distinguished Boodle's. Had never received an invitation to any Society
ball or soirée or dinner party, or if so, had certainly
never accepted it.

The "offer" Heath referred to was an increasingly
desperate attempt to buy out Bryony's portion of his
vice establishment.

Not that he had any idea a woman was involved.

No one ever did.

Long before she was out of the schoolroom, Bryony would sneak into her father's office whenever he
was from home, and pore over his financial journals
and the business reports he would receive on his investments.

With no one to guide her, at first it had been con-
fusing. Quickly, however, she began to recognize
patterns of risk and reward, of volatile markets and
conservative investments, of all the untapped potential of the opportunities Father did *not* take.

She hadn't been able to resist trying her hand.

Heath had helped her pawn several possessions
of value to create that first nest egg. Bejeweled tiaras
she'd received as gifts, sumptuous gowns she'd
grown out of, the monthly pin money she'd been sav-
ing for most of her life. The sum wasn't as much as
she would have liked, but a few high-risk, high-re-
ward, short-term ventures later, it had begun to look
mighty respectable.

She hadn't been in a position to fund fleets of

cargo ships or open textile factories, but when the opportunity arose to cover the initial costs for a fledgling gambling hell in exchange for ten percent of the monthly income until it repaid the original debt at a twenty percent profit, with a one percent stake for the first five years—well, she'd have been foolish not to take it.

In fact, she was still baffled at having been given the chance at all. So many other investors could have easily taken her place, yet had overlooked the opportunity completely.

Featherwits, all of them.

The original contract had stated that if Maxwell Gideon did not settle the debt in full within five years, Bryony would receive fifty percent of the monthly profits instead of twenty. He had repaid the money within two years.

His only mistake was underestimating Bryony.

Gideon had been focusing so hard on the goal of escaping a five-year contract as quickly as possible that he had failed to appreciate the value of the money his club was generating.

As the club did better and better, Bryony's one percent stake became more and more lucrative. Yet time was against her. Only a few months remained on the contract and there was no reason for him to sign another. So she had used her earnings—and a pseudonym—to purchase the land and property that housed the Cloven Hoof. A brilliant maneuver.

Before, the club's rent had been going to a third party.

Now, the money went directly to Bryony.

The moment Maxwell Gideon had realized his new landlord was none other than the silent investor he'd believed himself almost rid of, he had immediately offered to buy the deed from her at a rate ten percent higher than what Bryony had paid to procure it. Then twenty. Then thirty.

Now he had *doubled* the offer?

This was indeed an interesting turn of events.

"Well?" Heath asked with a droll lift of his brows. "Has that clever brain of yours calculated a decision?"

"Not yet," she said softly, her mind still whirring with possibilities. "More information required."

Her brother looked surprised. "Shall I request a report of some kind? I thought the terms of your contract required the Cloven Hoof to disclose details monthly."

"It does," she agreed. "Which is how I know the amount of profit it has earned. Given he's also had to finance his own life, Mr. Gideon would be forced to deplete most if not all of his current savings in order to double the offer. He either has more money than he has disclosed, or he is exceedingly foolish."

Heath shrugged. "Max wants to be full owner of the club."

"Understandable. But willing to give up everything for total control?" She narrowed her eyes. "It's suspicious, to say the least."

Her brother frowned. "You think he's hiding something?"

"Available facts would suggest that conclusion." She hated missing an important part of the picture. Especially when it came to finances. She would have to investigate. "I require a fortnight to perform an analysis of my own."

"Very well. I'll have the appropriate response drawn up." Her brother pulled a face when he glanced at the hour on the clock upon the mantel.

"Late?" she asked with sympathy.

"Dreadfully." Heath brushed off his trousers and rose to his feet. "Good luck with your computations. Try not to think too hard!"

And with that, her brother was gone. Bryony was once again alone.

But this was fortunate, for tonight's unexpected change of plans required solitude.

She hurried from the sitting room to her dressing chamber. With a few careful contortions, she managed to twist out of her gown. She did not wish to summon her lady's maid. Although the staff had turned a blind eye to the siblings' various antics for more than a decade, the fewer eyes upon her transformation, the better.

After quitting her shift, she reached in the back

of the armoire where she kept her well-worn collection of lad's clothing, and a strip of cloth to bind her
bosom. In no time at all, she was dressed in white
small-clothes, gray waistcoat, dark trousers, black
boots. It was all so much *easier* than lacing up stays
and fastening a hundred tiny buttons.

And, if her mother's rhetoric was to be believed,
the disguise was completely unnecessary. All a
woman had to do was step outside with un-curled
hair, and the entire world could be forgiven for believing her to be a man.

Bryony sighed. If she *had* been born a man, none
of her problems would exist. But that was not her lot,
and the only choice was to make do.

Or go undercover.

If costumes and pseudonyms were the only way
she ever achieved anything meaningful, then so be it.

She slipped into a sturdy black greatcoat that
shrouded her from shoulders to shins and strode to
the dressing table for some pins. Uncurled as her
plain brown hair might be, 'twas still best to keep it
pinned safely inside her hat.

When she was through, she turned to the looking-glass to inspect her handiwork.

The greatcoat was a bit too long, the hat a bit too
big, but together all of the garments served to hide
her form and shadow her face. It would do, just like
it had done many times before.

She shoved several coins, a tinderbox, a slip of

paper, and a pair of bronze keys into her pocket. Then she hurried from her bedchamber to the servants' staircase that led to the rear exit.

As soon as she reached the street, she flagged down a hack.

"Where to?" the driver asked without bothering to look over his shoulder.

"Cloven Hoof," she replied as gruffly as possible.

He didn't ask any more questions.

Bryony, however, was full of them. Why was Maxwell Gideon so determined to own the lot? Only a fool would spend such a sum on an overpriced property merely out of pride.

She slid her hand into her pocket to touch the keys. Bryony possessed a copy because she owned the building, but had never before dared to enter.

Thanks to both the scandal columns and her monthly reports, she knew the Cloven Hoof was closed on Tuesdays. Mr. Gideon and the rest of his patrons had quit the premises at dawn this morning, and wouldn't return until dusk tomorrow. All employees had the day off. The club would be empty.

Except for Bryony.

Excitement began to race through her veins. This would be just like sneaking into her father's study as a child. Better, even. Bryony had been far more scared of the baron's wrath than she worried about Maxwell Gideon. He would never even know she'd been present.

What Bryony wanted to know was whatever he'd left out of his report. Why offer such an extravagant sum for a small rectangle barely brushing the border of the fashionable district? She'd plotted the earnings trends time and again. At this rate, Mr. Gideon could afford to purchase a much better venue within a few more years. There was no reason to spend one's last penny on the current locale.

Unless there *was*. In which case, she needed to know the reason.

Now that her sister's school was no longer in danger of closing without Bryony diverting her personal income to save it, she was free to save or invest her money as she saw fit. The price she'd been offered for the property would be a welcome windfall, indeed.

It was also a short-term gain. If Mr. Gideon had no intention of relocating, she—or her future husband—would earn far greater returns by collecting rent month after month, year after year. The Cloven Hoof was doing a brisk business. Rent could be priced accordingly.

Of course, following that plan would inhibit her ability to engage in other opportunities requiring ready cash. There would be no way to know which avenue offered the surer reward until—

"Cloven Hoof." The driver pulled his horses to a stop. "Looks closed."

"Rotten luck," Bryony groused in as manly a

voice as she could muster, and flipped the driver a coin as she bounded from the carriage.

She did not pause at the Cloven Hoof, but strolled off as if she hadn't a care in the world.

The driver wasted no time in continuing on in search of his next fare. Only once he was out of sight did Bryony circle around to the rear of the club and place her ear to the door.

It was silent.

She slid her key into the lock and twisted. The door unlocked with ease. She held her breath as she opened the door.

Nothing.

The coast was clear.

Ever since she'd made the purchase, she'd studied the plans for the property, and could likely find her way about in the dark.

Nonetheless, she welcomed the moonlight streaking through a few high windows. It was impractical to bring a lit candle on a carriage ride, and she was glad to discover she could see—if dimly. She was standing at the rear of the long corridor that bisected the club's interior.

She inched forward with caution.

Mr. Gideon's office was to her left, a supply room to the right. Once she cleared these, she came to a small area with chairs and tables on either side. According to her monthly reports, this area was designated for conversation, not gambling. After this section was the primary salon, which contained a bar, dozens of gaming tables in a large open area, and a handful of smaller tables for spectators along the edges.

This last bit, she had to trust more to her research than her eyes. Very little light snuck into the front salon, likely to protect the gamblers' privacy from passers-by on the street outside.

A tenseness she hadn't been willing to acknowledge disappeared from her shoulders.

No one was here.

She was safe.

With a sigh of relief, she turned her back on the gaming tables and retraced her steps to the rear office.

She'd known the club would be empty. Past trends had indicated this was the safest of all moments to attempt a reconnaissance mission. All the same, she was relieved to be proven right.

After all, she well knew her disguise wouldn't pass muster in direct light, or if forced to hold a lengthy conversation. It was simply for getting about in the shadows. A protective shield from the night.

A lad alone never received so much as a second glance. A lady alone received far more than mere glances.

Bryony far preferred being the lad.

She unlocked the office door. Despite the utter blackness within, she locked the door tight behind her as soon as she stepped inside.

Although the plans of the building failed to indicate the location of candles and sconces, logic dictated that there must be one near the door for those entering or exiting the office. She retrieved the tinderbox from her pocket and struck the flint to the metal.

There. Quickly, she lit a taper and lifted the candle from its holder. She stared about her in wonder. *This* was the black heart of the *ton*'s most infamous den of iniquity?

A stately mahogany desk not dissimilar from her father's stood just opposite. A decidedly non-devilish bookshelf covered the wall behind it. Then three comfortable chairs, one behind the desk and two in front for visitors. On the wall facing the alley, a small fireplace. Parallel to the other wall, a comfortable looking settee and an ornate folding curtain, presumably to hide a chamber pot from view.

Also absent from view: coal, brimstone, hellhounds, loose women, or gambling accoutrements of any type. Indeed, she could spy neither a decanter for port nor a tobacco pouch or snuffbox. Not even a token bit of clutter.

From this vantage point, one might be forgiven for believing that the Lord of Vice indulged in no vices whatsoever.

She edged closer to the pristine desk. Not only

wasn't a single paper out of place, there were no documents to rifle through at all. The desk was completely bare. She settled into Mr. Gideon's chair and tried to imagine where he might hide secret information he didn't wish for his landlord to see.

The desk drawer? Too obvious. But she jiggled the handle anyway.

"Locked," she muttered under her breath.

Of course it was. Even if the drawer was empty, a man this slavishly organized would leave nothing to chance.

She let go of the drawer handle. Her keys only worked on doors, and forcing the drawer open would only leave proof of her presence. That was the last thing she needed.

Besides, who hid sensitive documents right where a spy would look for them? He was more likely to... carve a secret compartment inside a book.

She leapt to her feet and moved to inspect the bookshelf.

Samuel Johnson... Horace Walpole... *Vindication of the Rights of Woman* by Mary Wollstonecraft... Bryony blinked.

The idea of the powerful owner of an infamous vice den voluntarily reading female philosophies was so delightful that at first the distant voices down the corridor failed to register as anything more than background noise.

Voices.

Corridor.

Maxwell Gideon was *here*.

She leapt behind the folding screen just as strong footsteps reached the other side of the office door. Frantic, she blew out the candle and squeezed herself as tightly into the corner as possible.

As long as neither Mr. Gideon nor his guest peeked behind the screen, Bryony should be safe here in the shadows.

But if anyone did...

The door swung open and flickering candlelight filled the office with a dim orange glow.

Bryony held her breath.

From her position squeezed against the wainscoting at the opposite end of the room, her potential exposure was limited to the tiny sliver visible in the half-inch crack between the edge of the curtain and the wall. She could see a slice of the carpet, the desk, the chairs, but no glimpse of the man who had just unlocked the door.

Why wasn't he crossing into the room? Why had their conversation suddenly stopped? Her hands shook so violently that she nearly dropped the spent taper gripped in her trembling fingers.

Her heart thudded in horrified realization.

The candle. Of course. Anyone's first act upon entering a dark room would be to light the sconces therein, and she had pilfered the most convenient of those candles for her own purposes. She could still smell the faint odor of smoke emanating from the burnt wick.

Mr. Gideon must be wondering what became of the strangely absent candle. Perhaps he would assume his staff had removed a spent nub with the intention of replacing it with a fresh taper, before being distracted by some more pressing matter.

Or perhaps a man considered a devil in his own right would detect not only a faint whiff of smoke in the chill air, but also the panic emanating from Bryony's very pores. There was nowhere else to hide. Nowhere to run. Nowhere to—

"Sit," came a low, deep voice as rich and dark as warm chocolate. "It'll be warmer in a moment."

Bryony's narrow line of sight was suddenly filled with a man of impressive height, broad shoulders, then unfashionably long black hair curling against a snowy white cravat as he knelt before the fireplace.

Before she could glimpse his face, orange flames leapt from the grate. He turned away from both the fire and the folding-screen to stride toward the desk.

"I appreciate you hearing me, Gideon," said the other man, who had yet to take his seat as instructed. "I had nowhere else to turn."

"No one who sees me ever does," Mr. Gideon agreed as he settled into the large, imposing chair facing his guest...

Directly facing Bryony's hiding spot.

Glittering black eyes. Sharp, slashing cheek-bones. Full, sensuous lips. Blindingly handsome and breathtakingly dangerous.

A portly man with thinning brown hair minced into the seat opposite.

The folding screen blocked her view. All she could do was listen.

"Tell me everything," Gideon commanded.

"I find myself balancing on the edge of ruin," his guest began hesitantly. "Textiles are my family's livelihood. The building that housed our looms burned down last Thursday, and my wife and daughter barely escaped with their lives."

Bryony frowned. While she held a great deal of empathy for the man's plight—indeed, this was precisely the sort of case she favored when determining her own investments—what on earth did this man expect Maxwell Gideon to do about it?

Given his disclosed balances, the Cloven Hoof's total profit would barely cover the most recent offer Mr. Gideon had made for the property around them. There was nothing extra to donate to needy persons, no matter how noble the request.

"How much do you need, Schneider?" Mr. Gideon asked, his voice detached and dispassionate as if the emotional story he'd just heard was meaningless compared to cold, hard numbers.

"A thousand pounds?" Mr. Schneider replied hesitantly.

Bryony would have laughed, had his situation not been so dire.

She had commissioned an exhaustive investigation prior to agreeing to help fund the Cloven Hoof's development.

Mr. Gideon did not come from money. That was the entire reason why he'd needed her help in the first place. Five years may have passed in the interim, but Bryony was well-versed in the club's daily gains and losses. The Cloven Hoof was doing a brisk business, but not so brisk as to cover both the price of the property and a thousand pounds for a patron in need of alms.

"No." Mr. Gideon's harsh reply was cold and final. "You would need at least two thousand just to replace the machinery. We need to rebuild stronger and safer. If I choose to invest, I shall require ten percent of profits until you've repaid your debt at twenty percent interest."

She blinked. That was exactly the sort of devil's bargain she had first proposed to *him*. But how could he—

"Done," Mr. Schneider answered quickly. "Whatever you require will be my privilege to provide, Mr. Gideon. You've helped so many of us. Without you, there would be no hope."

He *did* have the blunt? That deliciously devious imp! Bryony's mouth fell open.

Although his pockets had been markedly empty

when the club first opened, he must have been using every ha' penny of profit he earned to invest in gradually increasing schemes in order to raise higher and higher returns.

By doing so under his personal name and after business hours, such private arrangements could theoretically be exempt from inclusion in the otherwise extremely detailed and candid financial reports sent to Bryony on the first of every month.

Not only must he have more than enough resources to purchase the deed from her... she no longer had any idea how *much* money was at his disposal, putting her in a very disadvantaged bargaining position indeed.

Moments ago, Bryony would have sworn that no man in England tempted her in the slightest.

Maxwell Gideon was far from naïve. He was resourceful, ruthless, and dangerously clever. A potent cocktail of characteristics that appealed far more than she preferred to admit.

She shivered in pleasure to realize the increased pounding of her heart had more to do with the intelligent, handsome scoundrel on the other side of the folding screen than the threat of discovery.

He was more than her intellectual equal. He was trouble in every possible sense.

She couldn't wait to find out just how much trouble. Firsthand.

Chapter 2

*M*axwell Gideon did not offer an encouraging smile to the nervous patron seated across from him. In part, because Max rarely offered smiles of any variety. More importantly, men like Schneider did not approach Max in his private chamber because they sought charm or politesse.

Men like Schneider were desperate. They sought riches. Or rescue.

Both were within Max's power to give—or to withhold.

"Tell me about your wife and daughter," he commanded. "Are they hurt?"

"No one was burned, but they spent days nursing wracking coughs. The smoke, you know," Schneider said hoarsely, his eyes downcast. "Without an income, I cannot help my family. We need a miracle and I have nowhere else to turn."

Of this, Max was certain.

While he had no firsthand experience of the sort of business transactions one might see transpire at gentlemen's clubs like White's or Brooks's, the very fact that only the titled and the well-connected were allowed within their hallowed walls meant common tradesmen like Schneider could not avail himself of their innumerable advantages.

The Cloven Hoof was no such establishment.

Max had founded this venue not to ape his betters, but to spite them. He had no interest in pretending to be part of their exalted circles. He wanted to be their equal.

Were their fancy clubs so exclusive that one could only gain entry if approved by all the ruling members?

How precious.

Membership to Max's club could be granted by one man and one man only.

Max.

At first, little attention had been paid to his shadowy gaming club just a few streets too far from the fashionable district. Once the dukes and earls and heirs and fops realized they must be *approved*, however, membership quickly became as sought-after as starched cravats.

He did not always extend his welcome to those born to privilege, and *oh* did that rankle them.

Max was happy to give their money to men like Schneider, however.

"We'll start with a small outbuilding," he began. "Once the first loom is in operation, we'll work on expansion."

Schneider sagged with relief. "Thank you, Mr. Gideon. You've no idea how much your support means to me."

Max had a very good idea indeed. That feeling of helplessness, of hopelessness, of scrabbling from nothing to scratch one's way toward something of one's own, to pure unadulterated *freedom*, was the impetus behind everything Max did.

The Cloven Hoof itself was the first and only tangible proof that he had finally achieved what had once seemed an impossible dream.

Or at least, it would be once he owned the property outright and was no longer answerable to any man but himself.

"Is there anything else I can do for you?" was all he said aloud.

Schneider hesitated, glancing around the austere office as if it were the first time he truly registered his surroundings.

One desk. Three chairs. Many books. One settee. No wine. No cards. No distractions of any kind.

Max did not allow them. His life was carefully ordered, deliberate and precise, every aspect exactly how he intended it. He'd earned it.

"You do so much for others." Schneider hesitated. "Oughtn't you to do the same for yourself?"

Max blinked. "The Cloven Hoof *is* for me. Everything about it is mine."

Almost everything.

Schneider shook his head. "You're here every hour of every day. Don't you deserve a life of your own?"

"The Cloven Hoof *is* my life." Indeed, Max was just getting started. His plans went far deeper than what was visible to the casual eye. He intended to expand his empire. Create an even larger bridge between two worlds.

"You can't marry a club or start a family with a stack of pound notes," Schneider insisted. "A wife—"

"Good God." Max reared back in horror. "You cannot be trying to *matchmake* me. Your daughter barely has sixteen years—"

Schneider blanched with an equal amount of obvious horror.

"Not to my Agnes," he choked out. "I meant... some other woman. I dedicated my entire youth to textiles and nearly missed the opportunity for something more. I wouldn't want to see you make the same mistake."

"I don't make mistakes," Max said simply.

The statement wasn't a boast. It was a lifetime of dispassionate, coldly calculated decisions. Logic, not chance. Plans, not unpredictability. He enjoyed being the master of his ship.

Schneider cleared his throat in embarrassment. "Please forgive the intrusion. I meant no offense."

"None taken." Max rose from his chair. "If there's nothing else..."

Schneider scrambled to his feet. "Just my abject gratitude. I'll commission the plans as soon as it's daylight. Thank you again. I'll see myself out."

Under normal circumstances, Max would not only have personally seen Schneider to the door, but also quit the Cloven Hoof himself.

This was the sole free day he allowed himself each week, and at this hour of the night he was running low on opportunity to do little more than catch a few hours' sleep before beginning anew.

However, tonight something felt... *off.*

A missing candle, when his staff was trained too well and paid too handsomely to miss obvious necessities like candles. One of his books, not lined up perfectly with the others. His folding screen, butted up against the wall instead of how he normally angled it.

His carefully predictable world was *different.* Max hated inconsistencies, no matter how small. He would put things to rights and then he could return home in peace.

He drew out his key ring in order to retrieve a fresh candle from the supply cabinet across the corridor.

Once the taper was properly seated in the wall sconce, Max began to feel better. Things were almost back to normal. Back to how they should be.

He ran a careful finger along the spines of his books to nudge them into alignment, then stalked toward his folding screen in irritation.

Who the deuce would have placed it in the far corner, when his entire staff well knew that Max preferred—

He yanked the screen aside and froze in surprise.

Also frozen in surprise was the wide-eyed lad hiding on the other side.

After taking one look at whatever thunderous expression was currently storming through Max's eyes, the lad blanched, flailed, and moved to flee.

Max was faster.

He allowed the screen to fall where it may in favor of grabbing the lad's thin arm and jerking the intruder further from the exit. Off-balance, the lad tripped backward over Max's feet and windmilled wildly in a desperate attempt to regain his balance.

Max reached out to intercept him before he cracked his foolish head against the edge of the mantel.

Before the interloper could make another attempt to flee, Max swung the wriggling lad away from the shadows and into the light.

Not a lad.

A *woman*.

Max nearly dropped her in shock.

In the space of a mere breath, his meticulously planned, carefully ordered world had spiraled far outside his wildest imaginings.

"Who are you?" he demanded without loosening his grip.

"Brian," came the immediate gruff reply.

Max doubted that very much. "*Miss* Brian, is it?"

An impressively unladylike curse whispered from her lips. Her eyes did not flinch from his. She was still pale, but defiant, as if it were he who had disturbed her plans for the evening, rather than the other way about.

"Let's try this again." His voice was cold, authoritative. "Who are you?"

"Bryony," she said at last. "Shall I address you as Maxwell or Mr. Gideon?"

Impertinent baggage. "Mr. Gideon. We are not going to be friends."

"How do you know?"

Max stopped himself from pointing out that he knew everything that happened between these walls because, clearly, his multi-year streak of controlling and predicting every aspect of his life, his industry, and his surroundings had come to a shockingly abrupt standstill.

He tightened his hold. "Who *are* you?"

"Bryony," she repeated.

But they both knew such an innocuous name did not come close to answering the question. *All* the questions.

Who the devil was this woman? Why was she in his office? Why was she in *breeches*? How did she get here? What the bloody hell was happening?

"You have yet to release me from your iron grip," she mentioned casually, as if perhaps he had failed to notice that she was still trapped in his arms.

She was reckless. Fearless. Fascinating.

No, he did not like it one bit.

"How did you get in here?" he demanded.

She lifted a shoulder. "The door was unlocked."

"Bollocks," he said immediately.

She did not reply.

He glowered at her in consternation.

The door had *not* been unlocked. He was certain of it. His staff was far too competent for such irresponsible behavior. They cared about the Cloven Hoof—and keeping their posts—just as passionately as Max did.

Yet what was the alternative? Some chit had happened to stumble across a compatible key in the back alleyway? She'd crawled through the coal chute? Slid down the chimney?

Very well. Someone had failed to lock the door. He would ensure the mistake never happened again.

"What are you doing here?" he growled.

She graced him with an angelic smile. "I adore gambling, which of course led to becoming curious about gaming hells. I figured if one were to tour such an establishment in person, why not choose the best of the bunch?"

Tour a gaming hell? He blinked at her bizarre, completely improbable explanation. And yet, something made him suspect her answer was closer to the truth than she wished to let on.

"Why?" he demanded.

"Why not?" She peered up at him from beneath thick, dark lashes. "Because I'm a woman?"

"Because you're—" Maddening. Unpredictable. Infuriating. Irresistible.

Max snapped his jaw closed and glared at her until he could settle on an appropriate set-down.

"—chaos incarnate," he finished, infusing his voice with as much disgust and disdain as such anarchy deserved.

She immediately brightened, wide brown eyes sparkling in obvious pleasure. "That is the most delightful thing anyone has ever said to me!"

Max stared at her in disbelief. "I was trying to insult you."

"That's partly what made it so diverting! No one but my mother has ever insulted me to my face before." She twinkled up at him unrepentantly. "Do it

again. Tell me my eyes are dull as dirt, my hips hor-
rendously mannish, my lips as boring as cucumber
sandwiches."

He was horrified to realize that the exact opposite was suddenly, appallingly true. Her limbs were
as delicate as a dancer's, her lips distractingly plump
and kissable, her warm brown eyes perfectly framed
by dark, coquettish lashes.

His traitorous body was far too aware of her in
all the most dangerous ways.

He released his hold on her as if her flesh could
scald. "I liked you better when I thought you were a
lad."

"You liked me!" She clapped her hands together
in approval. "I told you we were meant to be friends.
Although I must admit, you do look…"

Max folded his arms over his chest and glared at
her in silence.

He looked what? Common? Like the son of a
dockworker and an immigrant? He was proud of who
he was and where he came from, and certainly did
not need some moppet in men's breeches with a privileged accent to worm her way into his private
territory, only to—

"—less demonic than advertised," she finished
with an irritated sigh.

He found himself at a complete loss for words.

She dug a folded scrap of foolscap from her coat
pocket and tossed it onto his desk in disappointment.

"I was hoping for hooves."

The caricature.

A few months earlier, he had become the object of an anonymous caricaturist's pen. He had been depicted as the overlord of a hellish den of vice. Flames licked from the edges of the sketch, highlighting the manic faces of the gamblers surrounding him as well as a tell-tale pair of cloven hooves where his boots ought to be.

The symbolism was far from subtle, even without the biting caption: *The road to me is paved with gold intentions.* Thousands of damning prints had circulated London in a matter of hours.

Was that why she was here? To see for herself if he were man or demon?

He tilted his head and considered her.

As both the owner of a gaming hell and a man who had survived despite every obstacle thrown in his path, Max was well used to having to make quick judgments about those he came in contact with.

He could recognize both thieves and thief-takers at a hundred paces. Had avoided knives in the back both metaphorical and physical. Had become associates with the unlikeliest of individuals. The enemy of those who sought to destroy him.

Despite the ignominious circumstances of their meeting, the young lady before him seemed eccentric, but solid. His muscles relaxed. This woman's motives were unclear, but she was neither a thief nor a knife-wielder. The impression she gave was of someone looking for a friend, not trouble.

None of which meant she was welcome in Max's club.

She threw herself atop his overstuffed settee as if she belonged there. "Are you wondering who I am?"

"I'll presume...a very confused and lost young lady," he ground out.

"The trousers didn't trip you up one bit," she agreed approvingly. Her brow creased and her expression turned pensive. "I knew there was no point to wearing stays. Or bothering with side curls."

"Is there ever a point to stays?" he asked sarcastically. "You look ravishing."

She bolted upright. "*Are* you thinking of ravishing me?"

"I am not thinking of ravishing you," he bit out in exasperation.

Her eyes widened. "You don't ravish women?"

"I ravish plenty of women," he assured her, no longer certain what exactly they were discussing.

She tilted her head. "Just not me?"

"Not you," he said firmly. "I'm still leaning toward tossing you out on your ear."

"It *is* the breeches," she murmured to herself. "I shall wear them always."

"A practical choice," he agreed. "Particularly if you intend to make a habit of being tossed out on your ear."

"It's never happened," she admitted with a be-mused smile. "You cannot imagine how surprising this evening has become."

Max nearly choked in reply.

She was the one who could not imagine the mael-strom in his mind. He was not used to not having the upper hand. Not used to dealing with a woman like her. Not certain he'd ever met *anyone* like her.

Or what to do about it, now that he had.

She was over-confident, over-familiar, unpre-dictable. She had disordered his orderly world from the moment she flailed into his arms. She was a dis-traction he absolutely could not afford.

And she was reclining on his settee.

Suddenly, she consulted a small pocket watch and leapt to her feet.

"Late to the ball, Prince Brian?" he asked.

"Something like that." She made her way toward the exit without a backward glance.

"Don't come back," he called behind her.

At that, she turned around with a knowing smile. "You'd miss me."

As he watched her disappear, he feared her words were a curse.

Chapter 3

*M*ax was normally not the sort of gentleman to waste any percentage of his time on an activity as frivolous as shopping for a new waistcoat.

Max was normally not a gentleman at all.

He did not read Society papers or attend *ton* events. The only aristocratic faces he would recognize were of the individuals who visited his club. Any lordlings unwilling to mix with other clientele weren't worth a second thought.

Finding himself striding down the bustling St. James shopping district in the middle of the afternoon was as surprising to Max as it was to the fashionable set streaming past him.

To some, he was a ruler of the underworld, lord of a dark domain on the wrong side of respectability, a man who blossomed at night and belonged to the shadows.

To the others, he was no one.

An unrecognizable stranger not of their class, perhaps not worthy of notice at all. A certain swarthiness that bespoke time spent out in the elements. A certain burliness that came not from a gentlemen's sparring club, but rather from manual labor of some kind.

An arrogance in his stride and pride in his carriage inexplicable to those borne from generation after generation of gentility and wealth.

"Mr. Gideon!" A gentleman in an impeccable suit much too fine for inclement weather clapped Max on the shoulder as he passed by. "Good to see you out and about for once!"

"Mr. Scott," Max responded evenly. It was good to see the man sober for once.

Although known throughout London as the Lord of Vice, Max took great pains never to over-indulge. He preferred to rule vice, rather than be ruled by it. It was the only way to be master of his domain. And he needed to be the master.

But what had started out as a scheme to make easy money had become complicated when Max not only was good at and enjoyed his work, but also began to get to know his wealthier patrons. Many turned out to be decent men. Some even ended up becoming friends.

But then there were the others.

Despite the path he'd forged for himself, despite a lifetime of cunning and sacrifice that had culminated this close to success, his method of achieving financial security ensured his permanent position in the fringes well outside Polite Society.

Even the endlessly mocked and pitied *nouveau riche* enjoyed a higher level of tolerance—if not acceptance—amongst the upper classes.

Max did not care. He had no wish to make a leg to the patronesses or bow and scrape before some blithering idiot eighth in line to an earldom.

He wasn't even certain why the devil he was in the market for a new waistcoat all of a sudden.

Certainly it had nothing to do with yesterday's chance encounter with a lad who had turned out to be female. He shook his head.

He'd had a long talk with his employees about checking twice before leaving to ensure all doors and windows were locked. There would be no more surprise visits from eccentric young women. No matter how intriguing she might be. They were now unlikely to cross paths again.

For now, all that mattered was the Cloven Hoof. Once he owned the property, he would be beholden to no one but himself, and finally in a position to consider new changes in other aspects of his life.

Until then, he would focus the entirety of his concentration on acquiring the deed.

"May I help you?" asked the shopkeeper.

The deed, and perhaps a new waistcoat.

Max glared at the endless rows of expensive cloth winding through the haberdashery like a blindingly gaudy serpent.

All of the jackets and trousers in his armoire were the same color: coal black. His shirts and cravats, white. His waistcoats, silver or gray. Practical, predictable, easy. Why turn the simple task of dressing oneself into some sort of stressful, nerve-wracking gauntlet?

"Are you searching for anything in particular?" the shopkeeper tried again.

Max frowned. *Was* he searching for something in particular? And if so, was the item he was searching for something that could be procured by way of a St. James haberdasher?

"I need a new waistcoat," he announced. "Something fashionable."

The shopkeeper brightened. "We've just received a new silk in the most dashing shade of puce—"

"No puce."

"Perhaps a brighter shade? More of a mauve or a vermilion?"

"No."

"Yes, I see. Let's stay out of the reds, shall we? Over this way, we have a stunning turquoise and chartreuse blend—"

Before Max could open his mouth, the shop-keeper had already changed course.

"You're absolutely right. With your... unique de-meanor, you wouldn't require loud colors to stand out from the crowd. Although you may find our se-lection of browns and grays here in the back to be significantly smaller in number, I assure you these selections are every bit as rich and tasteful as their colorful counterparts."

Max sighed. Had he really come all this way to purchase an item of clothing completely indistin-guishable from every other waistcoat in his wardrobe?

"Do you have... less colorful colors?" he asked hopefully.

"Of course," gushed the shopkeeper without so much as blinking. He made an abrupt turn down the labyrinthine path and motioned for Max to follow. "A man like you naturally finds brown far too boring and chartreuse much too bright. Your particular col-oring is best suited for jewel tones."

Max followed skeptically.

With a flourish, the shopkeeper unveiled two hidden reams of fabric.

"Some customers feel the deep tones on the left too dark to be sapphire. The menacing blue of mid-night, not midsummer. Its warring hues evoke storm clouds over the ocean, shadows beneath the sea. You seem the sort of man who would embody such a shade, rather than be overpowered by it."

Max stepped forward, intrigued despite himself.

"The other option is what's meant to be an emerald of royalty, of princes and kings, but as you can see, its complex character goes even further. This green is a dragon's underbelly, powerful and vulnerable. The green of battlefields, not lucky clovers. A jade that wars would be waged over. The color of—"

"I'll take both," Max interrupted decisively.

He was fairly certain the shopkeeper invented his descriptions out of whole cloth depending on the client in question, but such clever improvisation only cemented Max's respect further. Reading other people despite their best efforts to keep their thoughts private was a skill Max himself practiced every day.

And the shopkeeper was right. Max was not the sort of gentleman who desired to stand out in lime greens and spangled blues. His puppet-mastery was orchestrated from the shadows.

Storm clouds threatening the calm of the ocean, dragon scales protecting a fearless beast... What owner of an underworld gaming hell *wouldn't* wish to associate himself with such imagery, even if it was all in his mind?

The shopkeeper gathered the reams into his arms. "Shall I send a few yards of each directly to your tailor or would you like to commission the final garments here?"

"I'll take the fabric with me."

"Of course." If the shopkeeper found this request unusual, he showed no sign. "I'll wrap up your order immediately."

In moments, the fabric was cut and wrapped, the transaction completed, and Max was out of the shop and back out beneath the overcast sky. He took the first hack he could find straight to his sister's door.

"Max!" Frances's tired eyes lit with pleasure as she welcomed him into the humble apartment Max had finally procured for her after years of bitter arguments over who should pay for what.

"Mouse!" he replied with equal pleasure, as he threw himself onto the least-comfortable of the worn furniture in order to allow his sister the better cushion.

In actuality, Frances was nobody's mouse, but as she was already the strongest, most stubborn woman of Max's acquaintance, it would not do at all to let on just how much sway she held over her elder brother.

He tossed his recent purchase to the threadbare rug at her feet. "I need a new waistcoat."

"You already own six identical waistcoats," she said without bothering to inspect the package. "I cannot possibly get to it in the next fortnight. Madame Drouart has me hemming an apparently endless trousseau for—"

"Green," Max interrupted. "And blue."

"Liar." Frances shoved her seamstress-for-hire work aside and reached for the carefully wrapped package at her feet.

"I'll pay twice as much as Madame Drouart's trousseau."

"The trousseau is for a Miss Rosenthal, and you won't pay a penny more than the current rate."

"What would Madame Drouart charge Prinney?"

"You aren't Prinney," Frances pointed out wryly. "Besides, I've no doubt hemming the Regent's unmentionables is such a privilege, I should be expected to do so for free."

"Then I shall pay whatever the prince's rate *should* be." Max gestured toward his purchase. "Open it."

With painstaking care so as not to damage any part of the paper, Frances unwrapped the parcel to reveal twin pools of dragon-scale-green and ocean-storm-blue within.

"Oh, Max," she breathed, as she pressed the rich softness to her chest. "These are beautiful. You are truly going to wear colors again?"

He waved away this line of questioning before it could turn to the past. These days, he made it a point to focus on nothing but the future.

"I suppose I shall wear them a fortnight or two from now," he said instead. "Depending on your agenda."

"I'll start tonight," Frances said immediately.

"If you start a single moment ahead of schedule, you must charge me an additional premium," Max reminded her. "If there is no time for new projects, then there is no time for new projects. I will never speak to you again if I catch you destroying your fingers or your eyesight staying up all night hunched over a single candle to sew without cease."

He did not add the word *again*, because neither of them had forgotten her chapped, engorged fingers or the terror of having to bind her eyes for a week in the hopes of restoring her ruined vision.

That was when he had plucked her from the hellish textile dungeon where she traded her health for a worn cot and a few pennies, and installed her in the safest, most comfortable apartment he could afford.

Frances had only allowed such highhandedness because she had been both medically blindfolded and drowsy on laudanum at the time. She'd refused to accept anything that remotely smacked of charity ever since.

He supposed they were far more alike than either wished to admit.

"I will start this very night," Frances said again, her voice firm. "Do not worry, brother dear. I have learned not to take on more than I can handle."

Max hoped that was true. Nonetheless, he would be sure to drop in as often as possible. Seeing family was good for both of them.

"Where did you find such exquisite fabric?" his sister asked.

Frances worked with equally beautiful fabric

every single day. She did not want to know who had
sold it to him. She wanted to know if Max himself had
managed to escape his cave long enough to see the
sunlight.

"St. James Street."

Frances nodded. "Of course. That's where all fine
underworld gentlemen do their shopping."

Max lifted his shoulder. Before he'd opened the
Cloven Hoof, he would not have been able to afford
such an expenditure. Not without giving up something even more dear, like candles or food.

But those days were done, or nearly so. He had
money, he had fame—or at least infamy—and once
he owned his property outright, he would achieve a
level of success that had once seemed impossibly out
of reach.

"St. James Street," his sister murmured, her gaze
far away. "When you're out there amongst them,
does it still feel like looking through a window at another world? As if scant inches separate you, but your
nose and fingers can only press against a pane of un-
breakable glass?"

It was a rhetorical question. The world had always felt like that for both of them. But he was *so*
close. As soon as Max broke free from his chains, he
would find a way to do the same for his sister. She
deserved it.

Frances wasn't lesser or unworthy or a poor little
dear. She was a fighter. Stubborn. Indefatigable. Her

faith in him had never wavered, not even in the darkest times. He would find a way to lift them both into the light.

"You should ask for more money," he said.

"You already pay far more than the market—"

"Not from me. From your patroness. You are more than a seamstress. You are an artist, and she knows it. She cannot afford to lose you. Your wages should reflect that."

Frances let out a low breath. "I do earn more than any other."

Making more than the others was a bittersweet accomplishment when one's employer would be just as happy to pay her employees in gruel. Frances' salary was barely enough to live on. Likely by design.

Both their parents had fought that war. Hard workers, dedicated, loyal, clever, punctual, exhausted. He was far too late to save their parents, but he would not allow his sister to follow them into an early grave.

"You shouldn't be anyone's assistant," he told Frances for the hundredth time. "You should be a modiste. You should have your own shop, your own clients."

"I don't want my own shop. I would like to sew less, not to be responsible for more."

Max's jaw tightened. "If you would just let me—"

"No." She pushed him away. "I will earn my own freedom just as you have earned yours."

"Frances," he began.

She folded up the fabric. "Come to think of it, I sit at peace in my home far more often than you are in yours. Weren't you going to hire a manager or two? Let someone else wrangle the club from time to time so that you do not have to spend every waking moment within its walls."

"I will," he promised. "Just as soon as I have the deed. Then my budget will be mine to do with as I wish. I have everything planned."

It wasn't just a matter of Max needing to own the property outright. If the current owner should choose not to sell, Max would be beholden to him forever. Or worse, the owner could decide not to rent the space at all. Tear it down, perhaps.

Max needed *this* location. Everything hinged on it. This street, this exact block, marked the border between the haves and the have-nots. This unassuming section of road and brick was the dividing wall that kept everyone in their place. Once Max had his way, the Cloven Hoof would become the gateway to allow passage between. A physical crossroads where all minds and backgrounds could blend.

But so far, the owner had ignored every single request to meet.

No doubt Max's livelihood mattered little to whomever owned the deed. Some aristocrat, most likely. A titled lord who couldn't be bothered to attend to the goings-on of a gaming hell. Perhaps some second or third son, whose idle hours were too filled with fashion and women and spending the bottom-less family purse to bother reading the missives and meticulous reports Max compiled every month.

Frances wiped a strand of hair from her fore-head. "I wish I could see your club."

"Women aren't allowed in gentlemen's clubs," Max said automatically. Except, he had just discov-ered a loophole to that rule, had he not? "That is, I could bring you by some morning before we open, if you like."

Frances shook her head. "I've seen my share of empty tables and silent rooms. I wish I could see it when full to capacity. Do earls truly sit at the same whist table as those who work in trade?"

"Every time." Max grinned with subversive pride.

He could have opened any kind of establishment, but he'd chosen the sort most likely to bring together people who would not otherwise be in contact with each other.

His shadowy nook was the great equalizer. In-side the Cloven Hoof, the men with power were not just dukes and viscounts, but rather to whomever Max had granted entrée. Worth depended on the turn of a card, not the title of one's ancestors.

Anyone who did not abide by Max's rules would be shown the door and told never to return.

Outside those walls, however...

No. He would not think about things he could not control. All that mattered was securing the Cloven Hoof's future. Once he possessed the deed, it would have roots. It would belong. And so would he.

And then he could find a way to help Frances.

He gazed over her shoulder at the narrow line of books above her mantel. His sister might refuse charity out of hand, but Frances had never in her life refused a book.

"Read that boring tome about botany yet?" he asked.

Her eyes lit up. "Twice. You seem more *atropa belladonna* than *conium maculatum* to me."

"You do have a way with words."

As talented as Frances was with needle and thread, her quick and clever mind was her true gift. She would make an excellent governess... if only she had been born into a high enough class to qualify.

She had no references. She'd never even had a governess of her own. No one but Max knew how smart she was, how valuable, how wasted her untapped potential.

He gazed over at his sister. Women like Frances never got the credit they deserve. The opportunities they deserved.

But neither of them would ever stop fighting.

Her eyes brightened. "When your club becomes self-sufficient, are you finally going to settle down and take a wife?"

"If I find the right woman," he replied noncommittally.

Frances laughed. "How will you meet any women at all if you never leave your gaming hell?"

Bryony's image flashed into his mind. He pushed it away, as he had every time since yesterday.

She was exactly the wrong sort of woman. Direct. Challenging. Invigorating. Big brown eyes and lips that begged to be kissed. A woman like that would—

"Who are you thinking of?" Frances demanded. "Right now. I can see it in your face."

"No one," Max said quickly.

Trespassing and eavesdropping were unforgivable offenses. No matter how intriguing and comely the woman.

Max rose to his feet before his sister could ask any more impertinent questions.

"Almost dusk," he said and reached for his hat. "I've a gaming hell to attend to. I shall leave you to your sewing. Try to get some rest."

As she returned her handiwork to her lap, Frances's shrewd gaze did not waver.

"Whatever you're running from," she intoned as if it were a curse, "I hope she finds you."

Chapter 4

*A*nother day, another soirée. Another six hours before Bryony could escape the monotony and go back out in search of adventure.

Her mother's elbow jabbed into her ribs. "There's the Duke of Courteland. Go speak with him."

"We haven't been introduced," Bryony hissed back.

"Then find someone who can make the introductions." Mother rapped Bryony on the shoulder with her painted fan. "Hurry, before someone else nabs him."

Teeth clamped together, Bryony pushed her way through the milling crowd. Not because she thought she had any chance of nabbing a duke—or even achieving a formal introduction. But because if she had to listen to one more diatribe about why all the other debutantes were daintier and sillier and more romantically successful than Bryony, she was certain she would scream.

Nonetheless, she performed her part. If her only way out of a betrothal to someone horrendous was to bring home someone slightly less horrendous but still palatable to her discerning parents, then she could not afford to waste any more time.

And yet, the only man she could think about was Max.

He was so deliciously overwhelming. Tall, strong, dark, powerful. She could imagine just what sort of vices one might get up to in his company. A man that intense had a way of melting one's knees, so that one all but swooned into his arms without any provocation on his part.

She had to remind herself that her investigation was into his business, not his pleasures.

"Miss Grenville," came a breathless voice from over Bryony's shoulder. "I heard the invitations to your upcoming family musicale had been sent, but neither I nor my daughters have received one. Could you please speak with your mother for me, at once?"

Bryony smiled and nodded, but there was no way she would be able to change her mother's mind about who would be allowed into their home. Now that she'd been given a finite date by which to procure

Bryony a husband, Mother attempted to limit the amount of competition at any gathering under her control in which Bryony and an unmarried gentleman might share the same roof.

The fact that Bryony would be on stage with her violin and not in the audience rubbing shoulders with the eligible gentlemen did not seem to enter the equation. Mother wanted all male eyes on Bryony and Bryony alone.

If anything, Mother considered it a boon that Bryony could not make a hash of things by opening her mouth and speaking.

"Miss Grenville," came another female voice from Bryony's other side. "What a lovely gown. Did I see that pattern in *Le Follet*?"

Perhaps. Mother's modiste kept Bryony's measurements on hand in order to send over whatever items her mother felt she should be cloaked in when forced to interact with Society.

"Who cares about my gown," Bryony deflected, "when yours is by far the loveliest in the room. Where on earth did you find such a becoming shade of violet?"

As expected, the delighted recipient of this compliment immediately launched into a detailed explanation of the origin of the fabric, the dye, and the fashion plate the confection had been modeled after.

Bryony smiled and cooed in all the right places.

Although she didn't know an Ackermann fashion plate from a Godey's, she had been playing this game for as long as she could remember, and could make High Society small talk in her sleep. Sometimes she feared she might nod off in the middle.

She'd been lucky enough to be born the youngest sister of the smartest, kindest, most talented siblings in England. Conversation with them had never been boring. She'd despaired of ever finding such a connection outside of her family.

And then she'd met Max.

He was clever and prickly. Antagonistic. Rough about the edges. He could not have intrigued her more. He did not scrape and fawn to her or anyone. He didn't have to.

His overpowering presence was capable of cowering others. He exuded danger. And yet he used his power and influence to aid those who lacked resources. Secretly. From deep within the shadows.

He was a handsome, arrogant contradiction. 'Twas no wonder he fascinated her so.

"There you are," came a jovial voice from right behind her.

She spun around and grinned to see her brother Heath and his wife Nora.

"We are heading to the cardroom to partner Camellia and Wainwright," her brother informed her. "Care to join us?"

Did she ever! Bryony's tight shoulders sagged in

relief. Not only had it been ages since she'd seen her eldest sister Camellia and her husband, playing cards was the Grenville siblings' favorite pastime. And an activity Bryony missed very much.

She reached for Heath's free elbow. "Absolutely."

A folded fan rapped down onto her spine.

"Absolutely not," Mother interrupted, stepping between them. "You promised to dance every set."

"I promised to dance every set for which I had a partner," Bryony pointed out, and lifted the dance card dangling from her wrist. "This is the first break I've had all evening, and the set is already half through. Certainly I could at least say good evening to my sister—"

"Invite her over for tea." Mother sniffed. "She and the earl don't visit enough."

Bryony gritted her teeth and turned back to her brother. "Give Camellia a kiss from me."

Heath gave her a commiserating grin, but escaped with his wife before he too could fall victim to their mother's machinations.

Bryony stared at their retreating forms longingly. The cardroom was overflowing with laughing faces, the dull roar of their chatter audible despite the orchestra in the other room. It seemed like heaven.

Even if it couldn't hold a candle to how she imagined the Cloven Hoof.

"Why are gentlemen's clubs only for gentlemen?" she murmured under her breath. "Someone should start a gambling hell for women."

Mother stared back at her in horror. "Never make such distasteful jests again. If you lack for entertainment, focus on your posture and your embroidery and get yourself married. That will cure you of too much time on your hands."

"Sounds marvelous," Bryony muttered.

Not for the first time, she wondered if it wouldn't be easier to make herself unmarriageable rather than find some Society gentleman willing to put up with her. But how?

Heath was right that the thought of playing the violin for the rest of her life did not call to her. But perhaps she didn't need to become a world-famous virtuoso in order to be unmarriageable. She could perhaps... run an alternative to Almack's.

Of course, she had no funds for such a project. She'd used the last of her money to purchase the Cloven Hoof property, which meant she would need to sell the deed to Max in order to fund her own venture.

She shook her head. It was a silly idea. Though to be sure, almost any idea was better than standing around this ballroom hunting through fops and dandies for her future husband.

"Here comes Lambley," Mother whispered in awe. "Straighten your shoulders. Smile. Don't show your teeth. Don't talk to him at all. Impress him enough to marry you."

Mother scrambled away from Bryony's side with all the discretion of a stampeding elephant.

"Miss Grenville," the duke said, as he offered an impressive show of leg.

Bryony dipped an equally deep curtsy. "Your Grace."

He affected a stern expression. "I was disappointed to learn you still have not accepted any of the invitations to my masquerades."

"I may have given one of the invitations to my sister," she admitted with a grin.

"Very naughty of you," he said approvingly.

Bryony's smile widened. Very naughty of Camellia. She had met her future husband at that masquerade. "May I have another chance?"

"Your name is always on the list," Lambley reminded her. "I'm still hoping to win back my money."

"Some hopes will never be realized," Bryony informed him sorrowfully.

He laughed and shook his head. "We shall have to see, won't we?"

She and Lambley had been friends ever since they'd first met several years earlier in a cardroom not unlike the one on the other side of this ballroom. Heath had made the introductions in order for Bryony to join him against the duke and his partner.

Lambley had nearly tumbled from his seat with

laughter at the thought of a seventeen-year-old girl being any sort of competition in a game of cards.

Twenty minutes later, when every penny on his person had found its way into Bryony's reticule, the duke had been forced to change his mind.

About women, about cards, and especially about surprise endings.

He had been fond of her ever since, although he thought of her more like a little sister than a marriageable woman.

Nonetheless, Bryony had failed to correct her mother's inaccurate assumption that a few exchanged words with the duke might become the basis for future matrimony. It would break Mother's heart to know that Lambley's true desire was for Bryony to teach him how to memorize the cards between every shuffle.

"When is the next masquerade?" she asked.

"In a fortnight," he answered. "Shall I save a place for you in the cardroom?"

She shook her head. "If I can make it, I will elbow my way in."

He bowed.

No sooner had Lambley left her side then a new shadow fell into Bryony's path.

"Talking to dukes now, are we?" brayed Phineas Mapleton, the most self-important member of the *ton*.

He was a bully and a gossip. The sort who made

rude, outlandish statements just to get a reaction. The only reason he was accepted anywhere was because his aunt was a Patroness and he was related to those with titles.

"Was that a duke?" she replied in a bored voice. "So good you were here to eavesdrop. Never say you don't have someone to stand up with you this set, Mapleton."

He snorted. "The only way someone would stand up with *you* is if you were in disguise at one of Lambley's masquerades and they didn't know any better."

Bryony cut him a flat look. "Who have I been dancing with, phantoms? This is the first rest I've had all evening."

"They just feel sorry for you," Mapleton scoffed. "Sparing you twenty minutes out of respect for your father is far more palatable than being stuck with you for the rest of their lives."

Normally, Phineas Mapleton's balderdash never managed to get to her.

Yet this one cut far too close to home. Her entire life, Bryony had heard she wasn't sweet enough, not biddable enough, not ladylike enough from her mother. Before, she had never cared. She was too busy having fun. Now that such days were numbered, she could not help but reassess her situation.

Would she ever find someplace that wouldn't treat her as an outsider and an oddity?

No. She would not let Mapleton win. She glowered at him in disgust. She didn't *mind* being who she was. He was the one who could not be tolerated.

"Don't wrinkle your nose at me," Mapleton said in pique. "You should mind your appearance. A face like yours is at its most attractive when hidden behind a violin."

"You'll never know," she snapped, as she curled her shaking hands into fists. "You have just lost the right to attend this coming Grenville musicale as well as all future Grenville functions of any kind."

"You shrew!" he gasped in outrage. "When I tell my friends—"

"Anyone who sides with you on this matter loses their invitation as well," Bryony said coldly.

He reared back in horror. "I cannot be the only one not in attendance. I shall be pitied!"

"I thought you were a stallion among pups," she replied innocently, referring to an unflattering caricature that had made the rounds a few weeks earlier, mocking him for boasting he was better than his peers.

His lip curled. "At least I'm not a lame nag, not even a tolerable enough mount to ride."

He flung himself about and marched off, nose held high.

Bryony didn't let her placid smile drop until he was well out of view. She had won that round, but it still felt as though she had lost. Mapleton was an insufferable blackguard and a plague on humanity.

But what if he was also right?

Chapter 5

*O*ne of Max's favorite moments each day was the feeling of peace and pride in anticipation in the hour before the Cloven Hoof opened for business.

He didn't see his gambling salon as an empty room, but as the twilight sky just before the stars appeared. It was not the calm before the storm or the last flicker of light before being engulfed in darkness, but a nexus of possibility, of promise, that rumbled through the walls and reverberated through the very air.

When the hack dropped him at the stones just in front of the Cloven Hoof, Vigo was already guarding the door. A movement at the window indicated at least one of the other employees was inside readying the interior for an influx of patrons.

"Did you make it to Vauxhall?" Max asked in lieu of a proper greeting.

Vigo's eyes lit up. "That I did. We adored the balloon launch. Thank you for suggesting it."

"Who doesn't love balloons?" Max asked with a smile.

Vigo raised his brows. "Did you attend?"

"Next time," Max promised and let himself through the door before there were any more questions.

The large, burly watchman guarding the entrance to the Cloven Hoof was almost as infamous as the club itself. Due to the requirements of his post, Vigo rarely exchanged a word of conversation with the hundreds of gentlemen—and not-quite-gentlemen—who entered these walls or were turned away at the door.

He was its drawbridge, its gate and keeper. Omnipresent, feared, and respected.

Max doubted it had occurred to anyone who had come in contact with Vigo to wonder what the man did when not lurking next to the gambling den's entrance. He suspected "attending balloon launches with a French poet" would not be high on the list of guesses.

Max would have to think of a way to include Vigo more. His post had to be lonely. Max sighed. There was so much still to do before the Cloven Hoof was perfect.

The original goal behind this particular vice den might have been to create a gentleman's club so exclusive even the aristocrats far outside Max's league would prostrate themselves trying to gain entrance. The secondary goal of ensuring men of high and low background interacted within these walls as equals had succeeded far better than Max had dared to hope.

And yet there were so many people still left out in the cold. The not-quite-gentlemen with deep enough pockets to gamble at the same table as viscounts and earls might be treated as temporary colleagues, but the man who guarded the door, the man who poured the ale, the man who swept up cigar ash and broken wine glasses, all of them were still invisible.

Maybe it was not possible to cross such lines. Perhaps it was a foolish dream. But Max would keep trying, keep pushing, keep smudging the boundaries that segregated people from each other.

Further on the list were men like himself. Men who didn't even count as not-quite-gentlemen. Sons of seamstresses and dockworkers, with the same amount of brains as anyone else but only enough coin in their pocket for a single round of loo.

Max's father had been a dockworker all his life. Every cent he owned, he'd given to the family, then gone right back out in the rain and the wind and the sleet to try to earn another penny. In the end, it had

killed him. Never a day off, never an increase in pay.
The titled toff who owned the dock never bothered to
check on his condition until it was too late.

Their mother was the reason his sister had
learned to sew. More than that, Mother was the reason there had still been broth to drink after their
father had died and his meager salary had stopped
coming. She had cried the morning Max left to work
on the docks himself, but had no choice but to let him
go. There wasn't enough money to go around, and he
was big enough to earn a ha'penny of his own.

And now he was halfway to his dream.

It wouldn't happen overnight, of course. Nor was
the current salon big enough for everything he hoped
to accomplish. That was why he had bid on both this
building and the neighboring property, which had
been under the control of a different landowner and
left empty to rot.

Max was happy to step in. In order to create a
communal crossroad between the workers and the
wealthy, the guests would need plenty of room in
which to intermingle. Significantly more space than
what the current venue could offer. Purchasing both
was an elegant solution.

The slender addition was smaller than the current property, but the shared wall dividing the two
meant that expansion was not only possible but inevitable. He would open the other side as a slightly

less exclusive annex, and then create interior walk-ways between the two to encourage visiting both sides.

Combining the two venues into the sort of establishment he'd always dreamed of running would be visible proof of success in an unfriendly world that had held his family down every step of the way.

But to do so, he needed *both* deeds.

Somehow, his extremely generous offer for the Cloven Hoof's land had been outbid without any prior indication of outside interest. Overnight, Max's straightforward plan had turned from a certainty into a disaster. The new landlord refused to sell, and the neighboring property was too small to serve as a replacement.

He needed both, and was determined to make it happen. But until then, he needed to keep his plans for expansion a secret.

If the silent investor had any idea, he would refuse to relinquish the deed at any price. Either to keep Max beholden to him financially, or to ensure such a mix of classes and backgrounds could not occur so close to the fashionable set's front doors.

Max headed straight to his office. He would write yet another letter requesting an audience with the owner.

His friend Heath Grenville had brokered the original contract that had enabled the establishment of the Cloven Hoof, and was the only person who knew the identity of the man whose purse strings had both granted Max's childhood dreams and stood in the way of achieving something new. Somehow, Max needed to break through.

He pushed open his office door and stepped inside. Familiar darkness greeted him. He lit the interior sconce just inside the door with one of the candles lining the corridor, then slipped inside for a few moments of peace before the day's work began.

"Minus ten points for failing to be punctual," came a bored female voice from the direction of the settee.

Max whirled to face the same woman in lad's clothing from the other night.

"Are you judging me like a horse?" he asked in disbelief. "Minus twenty points for disguising your body but not your voice, and minus one hundred for daring to return without an invitation."

"Fair enough," she agreed. "But I get a hundred-point bonus for realizing I was never going to receive an invitation and having the fortitude to come anyway. It all evens out."

"It's not even at all," Max spluttered. "How did you get in? Do not attempt to say the door was unlocked."

"The door was very locked," she assured him. "So locked that I couldn't get out. I snuck in with the late crowd before closing and fell asleep on your sofa."

His jaw clenched shut. He supposed he should be

grateful the person pointing out unexpected holes in his security was a young lady, not an arsonist or a murderer.

He did not feel grateful.

First thing tomorrow, his staff would suffer through a very displeased warning about checking the club carefully before locking up for the night.

"You should not be here." He loomed over her as menacingly as possible. Although she was obviously an eccentric and seemed to be harmless, she did not belong anywhere near his club.

She peered up at him with a sunny smile. "Says who?"

"Says the world. This is a gentleman's club."

"Mm, but isn't it *your* gentlemen's club? If you say I can be here, then I can be here."

"An astute observer might notice that I have said no such thing," he countered.

She lowered her gaze. "Do you want me to leave?"

"Yes," he said icily. "The lack of invitation was deliberate. Good-bye."

A knock sounded upon the door. "Mr. Gideon, there is an issue with today's delivery."

Normally, Max would invite his barkeeper in to chat about any issue that affected the club.

Normally, Max did not have an impertinent lady in lad's clothing reclining upon his settee.

He opened the door a crack. "What is it?"

A frown of confusion flitted across his bartender's face. "Did I hear voices? I didn't see anyone else come in. I can come back if you're busy with—"

"I'm never too busy to correct an issue. What happened with the delivery?"

"We were meant to receive two cases of Rioja and one of Madeira. They have bollocksed the shipment, and sent French wines instead. One Bordeaux, two of Champagne. It has doubled the cost. Should I send it all back? We did not budget for these prices. On the other hand, we cannot run out of wine."

Before Max could respond, his uninvited guest opened her mouth.

"The higher price is due to the trade situation with France, but that is also what makes drinking French wine so enticing. Accept everything and double the price per glass. Tell your customers it's 'victory wine,' or spoils of war. We beat Boney and will drink his land dry. Every bubbly drop of it."

Max ground his teeth together.

Bryony had kept her voice low and raspy, but if the barkeeper suspected for one second that the admittedly brilliant solution had come from a woman sequestered in the back of a gentleman's club—

"'Victory wine,' sir?" the barkeeper stammered.

"Go with 'spoils of war,'" Max said firmly. "Play up the plunder angle."

The barkeeper nodded. And tried to peek about Max's shoulder. "Who is—"

"My neighbor's nephew," Max said quickly, and all but shut the door in his barkeeper's face.

When he whirled to face Bryony, her countenance was not repentant in the least.

"Plunder! Of course. Far manlier than victory wine." She nodded at him appreciatively. "We make a great team."

He heroically refrained from shaking her. "We make nothing together because we are nothing together. You have to leave before clients arrive."

"No, I don't. I'm your neighbor's nephew. If I leave now, while there's no other clients to distract them, your staff will have nothing better to do than attempt to make my acquaintance before I exit the building. Once the nightly festivities are underway, they will be far too busy tending the crowd to worry about me."

"And what about the others?" Max growled. "The dozens of drunken men about to fill the gaming salon?"

"They don't know your neighbor's nephew is here and wouldn't care if they did." She quirked a brow. "The men who frequent places like this are in search of one of three things."

Max crossed his arms. "Which are?"

"Relief from one's creditors, power over others, or escape into a bottle. All of which have everything to do with themselves and nothing to do with me." She smiled. "It will be easier to slip out when capacity is at maximum than when I am the only outlier within."

Max did not dignify her assertions with a response.

There was no reason to. She was right and she knew it.

He stalked over to the folding screen behind his desk and carried it to where it did not belong on the other side of the room, in order to block any view of the settee from the desk or the door.

"Do not speak again to anyone but me," he ordered.

"Very well," she agreed quickly.

Max frowned. Her acquiescence had been too easy. She was after something else.

"Don't speak to me either unless I ask you a direct question," he commanded.

"Boring," she pronounced and propped her arms behind her head to settle more comfortably into the settee. "I am a distraction whether or not we converse, so we might as well take advantage of the opportunity to get to know one another."

He cut her a flat look. "What makes you think I have any wish to know you better?"

She arched her brows in amusement. "You are Maxwell Gideon. You own an infamous vice den straddling the best and worst parts of London. Both fishermen and dukes have been turned away bodily at your door. If you truly had no wish to get to know me better, I would already be out on my ear."

He glared back at her. "That doesn't mean I like you here."

"You don't know me well enough to know if you like me or not," she pointed out reasonably. "Let's change that."

"No," Max said simply. "I am everything you say, and the reason I have achieved what I have is because I do not compromise with anyone. I shall not start with you."

She thought this over. "You may not compromise your values or principles, but you make business arrangements whenever they are advantageous, do you not?"

He'd walked into that trap. "Not with strange women dressed up as fine gentlemen for reasons I cannot fathom."

"Can you not? I thought you were clever. Although you're right, I am strange. I've been told it's my best quality. And my worst, if you ask my mother," she added under her breath. "In your opinion, what should I have done to improve my costume?"

Max did not answer.

Her costume was not the problem. He had believed her to be a lad at first glance, and anyone who caught a glimpse of her from the corner of his eye would think the same.

The gruff tone she adopted when she spoke in no

way resembled an adult gentleman, but that too aided her verisimilitude. One could be forgiven for believing her to be a lad of an age where one's changing voice could not be trusted from one moment to the next.

But he knew better. There were curves beneath the boxy jacket, brains beneath the too-big hat.

The truth was, he was very much intrigued by the mystery she posed. What reason had she to take notice of fluctuating wine prices during and after the war? What gave her the impertinence to command a member of his staff, or the cynical practicality to have come up with such a solution in the first place? And why the devil was she here at all?

Before he could demand answers, someone rapped upon the door.

Max darted a glance at the clock beside his desk and held a warning finger toward Bryony. "Not a word."

She nodded submissively.

Max didn't buy it for a moment, but he had scheduled several private meetings and could not delay any further. Nor could he give any indication that there was a woman inside the Cloven Hoof.

He adjusted the folding screen one last time for privacy, then turned to open the door.

The next two hours flew past in a blur of worried faces with problems to solve. An investment here, practical advice there, an increase in credit for some, lowered interest for others. Presiding over case after case like a magistrate. Righting wrongs. Changing lives.

At last, one final patron awaited outside Max's door.

"Lambley," he said with pleasure. "Come on in."

The duke eased inside the office but declined to take a seat. "I didn't see you at the last party."

"It's a masquerade," Max reminded him. "How would you know it was me?"

"If you ever *accepted* one of my invitations," Lambley said with a secretive smile, "you'd know that nothing happens in my house without my awareness."

"I will attend," Max promised. "I've just been so busy here at the club."

"Have you considered hiring help?" the duke suggested.

Max raised a brow.

Lambley burst out laughing. "Of course you have. You consider everything. No doubt there's some scheme underway that no one will discover until you've chosen to reveal it."

"A scheme to keep myself overworked and exhausted," was all Max said in reply.

"Hmm." The duke toasted with his glass of port and turned toward the door. "If you need a diversion..."

Max inclined his head. "I know where to call."

No sooner had the door snicked closed, Bryony was already on her feet, eyes shining, hands clasped together in excitement.

"That was splendid!" She clasped her hands together and gave a little bounce. "You do this all day?"

"Speak to my patrons?" Max said dryly.

"Solve the problems of such diverse individuals," Bryony continued, undaunted. "A duke, a dandy, a sparring master... I did not know that there were places in London where such men intermingled."

"There aren't places," Max said with pride. "There's the Cloven Hoof. That's why it's important."

He crossed the office to sit behind his desk far on the other side of the room.

By the time his arse hit the seat, Bryony was already perched on the edge of his desk.

"Did you know that would happen?" she asked. "Is such a varied clientele something that can be planned from the start or was it more of a happy accident?"

"I hoped from the start," Max admitted. "Not everyone approves. The very effect you consider splendid is the primary reason why the Cloven Hoof will never be fashionable to the majority of the elites."

Bryony waved this away. "I'm sure it is the precise reason the rest of your patrons do choose to frequent this establishment."

Max tilted his head. He had assumed his customers considered economic diversity a tolerable side effect of the Cloven Hoof, not its best quality. He would love to believe that were true. "Why do you think so?"

"Who wouldn't?" Bryony squinted in thought. "In a place like this, chance encounters could spawn all sorts of complex conversations that would never have surfaced around a lukewarm bowl of ratafia within Almack's hallowed-but-tarnished walls."

Max shrugged. He had never been inside Almack's. "I couldn't say."

"For most of your clientele," Bryony continued, "I would assume your greatest competition comes from other gentlemen's clubs like White's and Brooks's."

"No," Max corrected. "Rich or titled gentlemen might have that option, but my other patrons do not. One must receive approval from thirty-five members of White's to join their esteemed rank. Here at the Cloven Hoof, the only opinion that matters is my own. No one can compete with that."

Bryony grinned at him. "How unapologetically arrogant. I cannot imagine why you are still a bachelor."

To his surprise, he enjoyed sparring with her. He raised his brows. "What makes you think I am?"

She leaned forward. "Aren't you?"

Max gave a half smile instead of a reply, just to

vex her.

He was indeed still a bachelor, though likely not for the reasons Bryony suspected.

Women did not reject him for his arrogance. If anything, his increased status and financial prowess only served to attract fortune-hunters. Max was uninterested. When he chose to take a wife, it would be a woman who wanted *him*, not one who sought to profit off of him.

He narrowed his eyes at Bryony.

What was she after? It was impossible to say. She did not appear to want anything from him personally, which implied rebellion or a search for adventure were the only reasons she continued to trespass where she didn't belong. He should not allow her to do so.

That reality was enough to douse any warm feelings he might have felt toward her. Being used as an avenue for rebellion or adventure was as distasteful as being used as an avenue to deeper purse strings. In both cases, the attraction was not to Max but rather what an association with him might offer.

"Very well," she said when he failed to rise to her bait about his marital status. "Don't tell me. I shall shock you by admitting that I find myself a spinster with little hope of wedded bliss."

"Not a spinster." He took in her long lashes, her high cheekbones, her soft skin. The only reason her disguise worked at all was because she was still young. Yet it only worked at a glance. Upon closer inspection, her beauty gave her away. "You cannot be more than twenty."

"Four-and-twenty. Now you see why my mother despairs."

"She doesn't despair because you are four-and-twenty," he pointed out. "She despairs because you gallivant about London unchaperoned in men's clothing. You'll never find a nice gentleman that way."

"Perhaps I don't want a nice one," Bryony said.

Max straightened with interest. He was very good at being very bad.

"Perhaps I don't want a husband at all," she continued indifferently.

For some reason, this rankled. "Why wouldn't you?"

"I see no reason to fawn over every man who stands up with me at Almack's. Being leg-shackled to the wrong husband would be a thousand times worse than not having one at all. How can I give them my hand if they can't even keep my attention?"

Max's flesh chilled to realize that her earlier comments about warm ratafia and tattered decor had been based on personal observation rather than idle gossip. Her vocabulary and accent indicated her education, but the well-worn lad's clothing had not hinted at wealth.

This new knowledge gave him no further insight

into what the devil a debutante would be doing in trousers and a waistcoat on the wrong side of town, but as strange a creature as she might be, he now knew her to be well out of his league.

Not that he should care. After all, *he* wasn't going to offer for her.

In fact, he was going to have another talking-to with his staff to ensure misplaced debutantes never found their way into the Cloven Hoof again.

Chapter 6

*B*ryony had no idea what she'd said to spoil the mood, but even she could see that she had done so.

Max's focus was not on her but on rearranging a small stack of journals that suddenly appeared to require the entirety of his attention.

Bryony tried not to be disappointed. Conversation with him had been so invigorating. She could not help but wonder what had just happened between them. The Cloven Hoof was a far cry from the sheltered sitting room she had once shared with her siblings, but for a moment she had felt a sliver of the same connection, the same camaraderie, the ability to just be herself.

Then in the space of a few breaths, Max had gone from tolerating her to ignoring her altogether. The awkwardness swirling around the silent room now felt more like her parents' drawing room. A place where Bryony was always either alone, or silently being judged.

But she was not at home. She was in the hidden private office of an infamous gaming hell, alone with a dangerously handsome man whom gamblers worshiped as a saint and ladies decried as the devil himself. And he was doing sums.

If even a quarter of the rumors of Max's unapologetic sinfulness were true, he could have debauched her three times over by now. Instead, he looked for all the world as if the column of numbers he was currently tallying was far more enticing than anything Bryony might have to offer.

She held her composure. It was not that she wished to be ravished by this tall muscular man with wide shoulders, tightly controlled composure, sensuous lips, too-long dark hair and even darker eyes that betrayed not even the slightest hint of what he was thinking.

Bryony had never been kissed, and she would rather start there.

She had not been *planning* on kissing the owner of the Cloven Hoof, but now that he was right in front of her, close enough to rub a finger along the rough whiskers shadowing his jaw, close enough to tumble forward into his embrace, close enough to slide her derrière off the edge of his desk and right into his lap, the thought of kissing him had simultaneously become the best and worst idea she'd ever had in her life.

She watched as he tallied another row of numbers. He did so briskly, efficiently, as fast as Bryony could have done herself, not in the least distracted by her presence less than an arm's width away. She could not help but be impressed with both his cleverness as well as his remarkable ability to shut the rest of the world out in order to focus.

Perhaps that untouchable aura was also part of his allure. He had always been a mysterious figure in society, and meeting him had only deepened the mystery. She had been terrified when he'd discovered her that first night. What if he had believed her to be a lad and beat her for her trespass? What if he had seen through her disguise and punished her quite differently?

The fact that he had done neither had caused her to draw an unexpected conclusion. For all his ostensible annoyance at her presence and her interruptions, she *did* feel safe.

She had inadvertently tested him under the worst possible conditions, and he had proven himself to be the sort of man who neither raised his voice nor his fist. He could have thrown her bodily from his club or told her not to worry her pretty little head about big scary concepts like "varied clientele."

Instead, he'd treated her like a person. He was

kind to her. Patient. Honest. Perhaps that explained why she felt so safe with him. Or perhaps when she looked at him, she too perceived more about him than others took the time to see.

"What are you doing?" she asked. By all appearances, he didn't give two figs about her one way or the other. He was no devil with cloven hooves and a forked tail, but he was still as untouchable. As unreachable. Even though he was right here in front of her.

She had never wanted to know another person more.

He slanted her a look. "Adding."

"Adding what?" she pressed.

"Numbers." He turned back to the journal. "Now I must start again."

"Three hundred and forty-six pounds, thirty-two shillings, five pence." She pointed at one of the rows in the middle. "I believe that's meant to be zero, not a six."

Max's gaze rose from his journal to her face. He laid his plume atop his desk and folded his arms over his chest. "You can tally sums over your shoulder from a journal facing the opposite direction?"

The back of her neck heated.

"Lots of people can do arithmetic," she stammered.

"No one but me has ever managed to read my

handwriting," he said drolly. "Upside down or other-wise."

Bryony swallowed. This was not the moment to tell him she'd had nearly five years of practice read-ing his detailed monthly reports. She would recognize his handwriting in any direction, under any light. She knew his hand as well as her own.

"I might've been wrong," she said quickly.

"You're not." His dark gaze stayed focused on her. "And you know it."

She wished she hadn't spoken. If she'd failed to tempt him by appearing in his office in breeches and a great coat instead of an evening gown with a damp-ened bodice, she would only make herself seem all the more mannish by continuing to correct him on his own mathematics.

She fluttered her hand in the direction of his journal. "I didn't mean to bother you. Carry on."

"You mean to bother me, or you wouldn't be here," he said matter-of-factly. "You might as well be useful while you're at it. Do you know what these numbers are?"

Her breath caught. Was he asking her to use her brain? Was he asking her for *help?*

Excited disbelief fluttered her pulse. She had dreamed of such a moment. And yes, she absolutely had a hypothesis about his numbers. Given the amount stated and the past history of income and purchases that passed through the Cloven Hoof, he was almost certainly tallying this month's beverage income.

But she couldn't tell him. That was something his secret investor would know, not something a woman who just so happened to slip into his club on a lark might be privy to. Despite the incredible opportunity, she still was not in a position to display her brain to full advantage.

Her responses would only be able to use whatever was currently perceivable to the eye.

"I haven't a clue," she answered, imbuing her voice with as much womanly femaleness as she could muster.

Max was unmoved. "Replacement candelabra. I'm switching from tallow to beeswax."

"Are you outfitting Buckingham Palace?" she blurted out. "The Cloven Hoof has no need of candelabra when the current wall sconces do perfectly fine. You already use beeswax candles. Either someone is trying to hoodwink you, or..."

Oh. She was the one being bamboozled.

He folded his arms across his chest. "How do you know?"

She cleared her throat. "If you had ever smelled a tallow candle, you'd know how I know. And I can see the sconces. Exchanging sturdy lighting fixtures for precarious candelabra would be a fire hazard once you add drunken elbows. Installing a glass chandelier worth any sum would be a waste on clientele who prefer the darkness."

"All true," he said after a moment. "Very observant. I'm more interested in why you would know the difference in price between various commercial lighting options."

"I am a candlestick-maker by day," she said without blinking. "Sneaking into off-hour establishments by night is only a diversion."

He did not smile at the jest, nor did he comment further on the obvious lie.

"Beverage income," he said instead.

Bryony hoped she kept her jolt of instant satisfaction at having guessed correctly from showing in her eyes. "Is the number good or bad?"

"All positive numbers are good numbers in this case." He glanced down at the list. "I'm hoping to increase them. I don't know if your idea to double the price of French imports will end up costing more than it gains."

Bryony did know. She'd studied the numbers. Not just his, but the books of all the other establishments in which she'd invested over the years. Numbers did not lie, and trends were predictable.

She moved her hand closer to the journal. "May I?"

His brows darted skyward as if the absurdity of their situation had finally hit him. A man feared and respected by the underworld and aristocrats alike, discussing hypothetical pricing strategies with a woman in trousers trespassing in his private domain against his will.

This time, his lips did twitch as he turned the journal around to face her. "By all means."

He'd *agreed*. Bryony's heart skipped, then seemed to beat twice as fast to make up. Other than her family, Max was the first man to treat her opinions like they mattered. As if her mind worked just as well as his. As though she were an equal.

The sensation was as bewildering as it was liberating.

Before he could change his mind, she lifted the journal and flipped through it in the hope that he had recorded the sort of detail she was looking for. The monthly reports she received from him were clear, but summarized.

She need not have worried. Within seconds, it became apparent that the journal she was holding was exhaustively and exclusively dedicated to the purchase, sale, and usage patterns of all beverages that had been consumed at the Cloven Hoof since its inception. She could not have asked for better primary information from which to defend her hypotheses.

"Here." She grazed her fingertip along the pages near the beginning. "And here, and here, and here." She skipped forward again and again, stopping only to point out certain figures. "And here, just six months ago."

Max leaned forward. "What are we looking at?"

"Those are times you raised prices on different offerings."

"I had to," he said with a lift of his shoulder. "My providers change prices and I cannot lose money on a sale."

"But that's the point." She showed him again. "You didn't lose money. If you compare sales numbers before and after each price increase, you'll see that there's no appreciable difference."

His eyes narrowed. "Perhaps I was fortunate."

"You weren't fortunate. You lost money."

He frowned. "But you just said—"

"I said there was no difference in raw sales numbers despite raising prices," she repeated. "That means, raise your prices. There is no difference in sales numbers."

He looked at her.

"Your customers come for the gaming," she explained. "They're here to spend money, not to pinch pennies. They're paying attention to their cards, not their credit at the bar. If they want a glass of ale they want a glass of ale. If they want a bottle of champagne, they want a bottle of champagne. No gambler who truly believes himself on the verge of winning a fortune gives a fig about the price of whatever wine he's swilling as he does so."

He stared at her for a long moment, then gave a

low chuckle.

Bryony's insides crumbled.

She had been too enthusiastic, too energized by numbers and profit curves and sales trends. Of course he could not take her seriously. She was a child playing dress-up. A court jester, not a financial advisor.

Max retrieved his journal and scanned through a few pages before setting it face down and closing his eyes. "I'm not fortunate."

Bryony's spine straightened. "What?"

He opened an eye in her direction. "You're right. I could have raised my prices long before my providers raised theirs. That journal records five years of profits that could have been much greater. I did not think of it, because I do not think that way. I am conscious of the price of every purchase I make. It's easy to forget that my patrons are not necessarily *like* me. Even if they are frugal in other matters, you are absolutely right. This venue is not a place where one wishes to mind one's pennies."

You are right.

The rest of the speech was pretty enough, but Bryony could only focus on those three little words. She was right. He had listened to her. He had taken her seriously.

He was the only man besides her brother ever to have done so, and this despite having given Max precious little reason to have any particular faith in her, mathematically or otherwise.

This was what kind of person he *was*. Tough, but fair. Willing to entertain differing interpretations of available facts before forming a decision. Willing to listen to someone like her.

Bryony's heart thumped. Max's surprising openness made her want to rise to the challenge even more, to give him a reason to keep respecting her.

"You're not unfortunate anymore," she said with a teasing grin. "Now you have me."

His expression hardened. "I do not have you, nor should you be here."

She flinched. He was right. She deserved that.

Nonetheless, she wished more than anything that the opposite was true. That he *did* have her. That she *could* be here. That together, they could create something more.

"You could have me if you wished," she said in a small voice. "I could be like a clerk. Off in some corner, unnoticeable until you need me."

Max shook his head. "You're not a clerk. You're a woman. This is a gentleman's club. You don't belong."

He was being truthful, not hurtful. And yet it hurt all the same. "It's your club. You make the rules."

"My club, but not my rules." He gestured about them. "This is what a gentleman's club *is*. Having a woman around, as a clerk or otherwise, would change the atmosphere in a non-advantageous way."

He was probably right. No, he was all but assuredly right. But she could not help but wish that he were not.

"Men and women have been known to get along," she muttered.

"Have they?" he asked drolly. "The only club where High Society men and women get together are marriage markets like Almack's, which is not the environment I am trying to recreate."

Nor was it what Bryony wanted from him.

What she suddenly, desperately wished, was that a place like this was available to a person like her. To women like her.

She didn't want to sneak into Boodle's dressed in men's clothing. She wanted to be able to attend establishments like the Cloven Hoof as herself. As Bryony. The eclectic mix of backgrounds and personalities and classes was more than refreshing.

It seemed heavenly.

She longed to be able to join in the conversations, the games, the teasing. Have an overpriced glass of port if she wished. By all accounts, the atmosphere in the Cloven Hoof was convivial and relaxed in a way she had never witnessed.

To many, this gambling den was home. A dark, shadowy nook that was positively welcoming to any gentleman worthy of Maxwell Gideon's approval.

But not to her. Never to her.

A knock sounded against the door. Startled, Bryony's eyes met Max's.

He motioned toward the settee at the opposite side of the room. "Behind the folding screen. Now."

She was already moving, flying off his desk and across the carpet to her predetermined hiding spot. Her blood pumped much too fast, her heart too loud.

The door creaked open just as Max was crossing to answer it.

"Situation up front," said a nervous male voice. "Afraid we need you for this one."

"Of course," came Max's low, smooth cadence.

The door clicked shut.

Bryony didn't know if Max had glanced her way before quitting the room. She didn't know how long he would be gone, or what he intended to say to her when he returned.

She was not going to stay and find out. She no longer needed to skulk about in search of secrets. The very first night, she had learned he possessed more money and far more brains than he'd let on to his silent investor.

Things were different now. She was no longer some pseudonymous landlord. He'd placed his journal of accounts in her hands. Trusted her more than she deserved.

With a heavy heart, she slipped out from behind the folding curtain, out of the empty office, out the darkened corridor. Whatever trouble was afoot up front meant that no one was minding the back. It was a perfect moment for escape.

Return to the world where she supposedly belonged.

Chapter 7

*B*ryony sat in the center of her mother's drawing room, stabbing a needle into white linen. She would much rather be reading a book, but the stories of adventurous men who are allowed to do whatever they wish had lost some of its luster. She was *not* mannish, no matter what her mother claimed.

She should not try so hard to fight the current.

Her mother floated into the room just as the butler arrived to announce the arrival of a friend.

"Lady Grenville!" squealed Mrs. Eastburn to Bryony's mother, as if finding the baroness at home in her own house at the hour of an obviously prearranged appointment had managed to both shock and delight her.

Bryony kept stabbing her needle through the

cloth as the two ladies bussed cheeks and comple-
mented each other on the handsome cut of their
gowns and the delicate embroidery on their bonnets.

Bryony had little to no experience with delicate
embroidery. Not wearing it, and definitely not creating it. She'd had to remove almost as many stitches
from her sampler as she put in, resulting in a swatch
of linen full of more holes than beauty.

'Twas probably fitting.

In order to give herself a project she would have
any interest in completing, she'd asked her artistic
sister-in-law to design a simplistic—yet demonic—
pattern comprising the words "Cloven Hoof" and a
few symbolic elements to remind Bryony of its iras-
cible owner.

It was not a highbrow endeavor, nor a work of art
that would ever be put on display, but it was expo-
nentially more amusing than embroidering still-lifes
of crooked fruit.

"That must be your daughter," Mrs. Eastburn
announced as if catching sight of Bryony for the first
time. But she made no attempt to speak to her or
greet her directly.

"That is indeed my daughter," Mother lamented
without so much as looking over her shoulder.

Mrs. Eastburn nodded knowingly. "The youngest?"

"The spinster," came Mother's long-suffering reply.

Bryony was suddenly grateful they were not addressing her directly.

"Come, let us sit over here where we will not disturb her." Mother led her guest to a clump of wingback chairs on the other side of the drawing room, presumably out of earshot.

The tall backs of their chairs successfully blocked their faces from view.

Unfortunately, Mother's idea of a whisper was still discernable in the otherwise silent house.

"What was I saying?" she murmured once her friend had taken a seat.

"It's what you didn't say," Mrs. Eastburn breathed in awe. "That one is the violin prodigy. Why do you have her here sewing samplers instead of traveling the world as a virtuoso?"

Bryony perked up. Perhaps overhearing hushed whispers wasn't a bad thing.

"All my daughters love sewing samplers," Mother said with the confidence of a woman who relied more on information plucked from the air and her own imagination than the empirical world around her. "And ladies cannot be virtuosos."

"She is a fourth child and on the shelf," Mrs. Eastburn reminded her. "I imagine she might enjoy the opportunity to do something with her talent."

"She has plenty of opportunity," Mother said. "The exclusivity of our family musicales is more than honor enough for Bryony. She doesn't need to work for money. She needs a husband. If you hadn't heard, her eldest sister managed to bring an earl up to scratch. I hope Bryony will do even better."

"A duke?" Mrs. Eastburn whispered as if this future husband was already a foregone conclusion. "Have you a certain one in mind?"

Mother was all too happy to expound upon one of her favorite subjects. "Of the two left in the Marriage Mart, I fear Lambley is almost beyond the pale. His infamous masquerades and endless debauchery would have to cease when he took a wife, else he'd risk exposing her good name to scandal."

"Or at least be more discreet," Mrs. Eastburn added. "One cannot consider his activities even an open secret when the man sends gilded invitations. Whatever happened to discretion in such matters?"

Bryony rolled her eyes heavenward. The Duke of Lambley didn't give a button what some baroness thought of his lifestyle. He had a large enough extended family that he could stay a bachelor the rest of his life if he wished without endangering the title. Lambley was free to live as he chose.

She quite envied him the privilege.

In the meantime, all she had to be grateful for was her quiet position out of view. Bryony had no wish to join Mother's conversation with her friend. The whispers her ears could pick up were teeth-gnashing enough.

"The Duke of Courteland," Mother was saying,

"is too new in his role for me to form strong opinions about him as a man, but perhaps that would make him the perfect husband for Bryony. Her father and I could mold them both into perfect pillars of Society."

"You are correct in all things," Mrs. Eastburn agreed. "Now that I see where your gaze rests, I understand your concern. Being a wife is a challenge and a duty. One cannot be a duchess and a virtuoso."

Bryony stabbed her needle back through the fabric.

She had no intention to be a virtuoso, not that anyone had bothered to inquire about her feelings on the matter. She had less interest in being a Society wife and even less interest in being a duchess molded into her parents' image.

And yet, she had no desire to be a disappointment to her family.

That was why she was sitting here in the drawing room, was it not? It was why she performed at musicales, why she danced every set at dinner parties no matter how badly her feet hurt or how dull her partner, why she was doing her best to learn how to create some semblance of order out of tangled colored threads instead of out exploring London. She hated being the child her parents could not be proud of.

Although her methods could be maddening, Mother truly wanted the best for all her children. She honestly believed even someone like Bryony held a prayer of snagging a duke. She expected her daughter to be the best she could be.

Even if it meant being someone else entirely.

"Do tell," Mrs. Eastburn began, once the tea had been served on their side of the room. They seemed to have forgotten Bryony's presence completely. "Has Courteland come to call?"

"He has not," Mother admitted. "No, don't look sorry for me. Our barony is respectable and our position in Society is sound. Bryony is far more presentable now than she used to be, but still not enough to attract a duke."

Mrs. Eastburn was silent for a moment. "Is it the hair?"

"It *is* the hair," exclaimed Mother, vindicated. "I've told her time and again that she will not catch any man without side curls, but she acts as if she hasn't the time to submit to a pair of curling tongs."

"She'll wish she took the time," Mrs. Eastburn said ominously. "If she ends up wed to a second son because she was unwilling to let her lady's maid perform the duties required of her, it will only be her own fault."

"I tell her so *every day*," Mother said with a groan.

Bryony gritted her teeth. Even though they believed her well out of earshot, she was not some mare at Tattersall's, to be discussed and dissected before being bid upon by gentlemen more interested in her outward appearance and capacity for breeding than in her intelligence.

But what point was there in saying so? Adding more fuel to the fire was not the way to win her mother's approval or gain Society's good favor.

Worse, from all she had seen, there was no reason to believe her mother did not have the right of the matter. Diamonds of the first water who bewitched earls and viscounts during their very first come-out were all of a type: the opposite of Bryony.

It went far beyond perfect hair, although even Bryony would admit the most successful debutantes did possess beauty in abundance. They were also sweet and biddable, accomplished in talents like country-dances and proper posture, with little ambition beyond giving birth to future ladies and lordlings.

They would not talk back or disagree. Their future husband would be a catch by all standards, and they were secure in the knowledge that their own worth was a fair match to his.

Bryony was opinionated and headstrong, quick-tongued and impatient. She rather suspected she would make a terrible wife, and could not blame any lord for not wishing to put her to the test.

The truth was, Bryony did want a secure future. She did imagine herself with a husband. She would love to have a nursery full of happy, confident children.

With luck they would be just as obstinate and opinionated as their parents.

Presuming anyone acceptable ever offered for Bryony's hand.

She lowered her gaze to her demon-inspired sampler. What *would* such a man look like?

Dark eyes and a sardonic smile rose to mind. She pushed the image away at once. Poppycock.

Not only was she far from the sort to fall in love at first sight, Maxwell Gideon did not inspire one to develop soft feelings towards him. Yes, he was sinfully attractive, and very well, she was consumed by the thought of kissing him, but those were desires one could quench in a single evening, not an attachment that would last for eternity.

She needed a husband who would make a place for her, who wanted her by his side, who would do whatever it took to be together. A partner. Someone who loved her for who and how she was, without exception.

More importantly, she did not want the sort of man who would send her away out of hand, who said *you do not belong* and meant it.

"What if," Mrs. Eastburn mused aloud, "we discarded dukes for a moment and considered earls and marquises as well. There are many more of them, which would give us far more opportunity to find at least one willing to take a chance on your daughter."

"It has to be more than a chance," Mother said firmly. "He must take her as his *wife*. Nothing else will do. I shan't allow him to play with my daughter's feelings."

Bryony sighed down at the crooked horns on her sampler. It was statements like these that she both loved and hated the most.

On the one hand, it proved that Mother truly did care about her happiness, and that she fully believed marrying Bryony off to some titled stranger would be in her daughter's best interest.

On the other hand, it also confirmed every suspicion that Mother hadn't the least inkling what Bryony's feelings on any given matter might be.

Possibly because she'd never listened.

"What kind of husband do you imagine for her?" Mrs. Eastburn asked.

"It has to be someone strong," Mother said, as if considering the options. "A weak man would be unable to mold her into the kind of wife he needs her to become. The sort of woman Society expects her to be."

Bryony rolled her eyes.

Even Mrs. Eastburn's answering murmur was skeptical. "How much can we reasonably expect her to change?"

"I am certain she is capable of anything," Mother said without hesitation. "She's very clever, with more

than just her violin. But she's also very headstrong
and requires a firm hand to keep her pointed in the
right direction."

Bryony's skin crawled. She did not want a firm
hand. And wouldn't the right man be pointed in the
same direction as she? Wasn't that how one knew she
had found the right suitor?

If her husband wished to mold her, to push her
into a predefined shape until she hardened in his image like wax, wouldn't that mean he had never
wanted *her* at all?

Once again, she could not help but recall her
most recent encounter with Max.

They had discussed numbers. Worked out a
strategy. He did not treat her like a silly girl, or even
like a man. He had treated her like an equal. Like a
fellow human whose ideas and opinions were worth
considering on their own merit.

And then he had actually done so. Had listened,
taken her thoughts seriously. He had not accepted
her words out of hand, of course, nor would Bryony
have respected him for doing so.

He had done his own calculations. And when he
determined she was, in fact, correct, he said so. Just
like that. No angst, no anger, no issues. Just *thank
you, splendid idea, I'll do that.*

Very well, those might not have been his exact
words. But it had been the sentiment. A sentiment

Bryony felt so deeply because it so rarely was directed her way.

It meant even more because Max was no fool. Every other potential investor had turned down his daring proposal because they didn't believe anyone could turn such a mishmash of ideas into a profitable club. He had done so in spades. Had proven them all wrong.

Instead of investing when they had the chance, all those naysayers now begged for the opportunity to walk through the front door and hand over their money. Delicious irony, that. Max knew what it was like to be underestimated. To be labeled without potential. A bad investment.

Perhaps that was why he was on her mind so much. It wasn't his dark good looks, or the way one must keep one's gaze fixed upon that wide, sensuous mouth if one had any hope of catching it in a smile. It was deeper.

They were more alike than she previously realized, and yet as much as they had both fought to carve their own paths in the world, they were still stuck inside the glass cases in which they had been born.

If and when he took a wife, it would be someone whose family would be proud of him, and vice versa. Who would rightfully believe their daughter had chosen wisely.

It would not be Bryony.

Chapter 8

*A*fter a long week of doing her best to stand up at every dance and flutter her eyelashes at any unwed, acceptable gentleman who chanced to glance her way, Bryony could not stay away from the sanctity of the Cloven Hoof for another moment.

Rather than let herself in a third time, she waited in the shadows until the last of the employees had left before rushing forward to knock on the rear door.

A sliver of moonlight fell across his face when he answered the door.

He scowled. "What are you doing here?"

"Are you alone?" she asked.

"Yes." He cast his glance over her shoulders at the vacant alleyway. "Are you?"

She nodded.

He crossed his arms in annoyance, but he didn't shut the door.

Her heart thumped. Perhaps she had a chance. "May I come in?"

His expression shuttered. "Bryony—"

"Please." She hugged herself to keep out the cold. "Just for a moment. It has been a tough day."

He wasn't going to allow it. *No* was written in his eyes.

"It's dark," she said quickly. "And late. What if I promise to leave at first light?"

This was blatant manipulation. He knew it as well as she did. Bryony had clearly made it this far across town in her tailcoat and top hat. Surely she could find her way back home in the dark.

Yet a true gentleman would be unable to turn her away.

Begrudgingly, he stepped aside to let her pass. "Dawn is in less than an hour."

She hurried inside before he could change his mind.

The week had been full of constant disappointments. Bryony simply couldn't please her mother. From the dozens of marriageable gentlemen who didn't ask for a second dance to the excruciating evenings filled with meaningless small talk about nothing at all.

Even if she didn't really belong, she felt less out of place hunched over Max's desk in men's clothing

than she did mincing about with her corseted spine
ramrod straight while forcing herself to giggle be-
comingly at inane observations about fresh scones or
rainy weather.

Yet she tried. For her mother. For herself.

At the Cloven Hoof, everything was different.

For the first time, Bryony very much cared
whether the gentleman in question happened to like
her back. Max had earned her respect. She didn't
want to lose his company.

"What was the reaction to the change in prices?"
she asked, as if she had any right to the answer.

Well, technically, she did have every right to
know, and would find out herself in the next monthly
report. However, that detail was not something she
could share if she wanted to continue to be received
with open arms. Or at all.

She was not just an investor, but the owner of the
land around them. A property Max very much
wished to regain for himself.

After which, he would have absolutely no need
for Bryony.

She *couldn't* sell. The entire impetus behind
sneaking in that first night was to discover whether
the deed to his property was worth holding onto. The
answer was obvious. Guard the asset and keep collecting rent.

Yet life was far from straightforward.

"Hmm?" he asked.

She cleared her throat. "The wine. Was there a strong reaction to the new prices?"

"As you suspected." Max scribbled in one of his journals. "No reaction at all. Except mine, when I saw our higher numbers."

Bryony knew that Max wasn't including her in his use of the word *our*, but her heart soared all the same. She had been useful. She had value.

If only she hadn't had to disguise herself to prove it.

She glanced down at her shirt and breeches and sighed. Even though she knew he would never have allowed her into the club dressed as Bryony-the-debutante, she wished he could see her as more than some strange woman in pants with an affinity for giving unsolicited advice.

For him, she suddenly wished to be *beautiful*. Elegant gown, hair ringlets, whatever it took to get him to notice her as a woman.

Yet this costume was the only way for her to pay him a visit. Disguised. Sexless.

It wasn't fair.

She couldn't come here to him as herself any more than she could attend Society events as her true self. At one, she disguised her outside. At the other, her inside.

How she wished Max could see through the layers to the real her.

"Faro or whist?" he asked.

She blinked. "Are you asking me to play?"

"I don't gamble," he said with a straight face. "I want to add some new tables. Which would be the most profitable?"

"You don't gamble?" she repeated in disbelief. "This is a gaming hell."

"No cards, no dice." He gestured at his obsessively organized desk.

"The Cloven Hoof *is* a gamble," Bryony pointed out. "You didn't know when you opened it if it would be a success or a failure."

"Maybe I didn't care," he said with a shrug. "Is it a gamble if the outcome doesn't matter?"

She narrowed her eyes.

The outcome did matter. Enough that he had used the only asset in his possession, his very home, as a lien. But no one knew that except Max himself, the potential investors who had reviewed his proposal, and Bryony's brother Heath, who had arranged the deal.

As far as anyone else knew, Max had burst onto the scene whole cloth. No one knew where he was from, where he lived, whether his entire financial state was wrapped up in the Cloven Hoof.

That was, nobody knew but Bryony.

"Where would you put the tables?" she asked. "Would you replace the seating in the sole area currently dedicated to drink and conversation?"

"Would *you*?" he countered and pushed a journal across his desk toward her.

She picked it up, fingers trembling with excitement. "You're asking for my help?"

"I don't need your help," he replied matter-of-factly. "But only a fool refuses to listen to outside opinions."

Bryony grinned to herself. He was right; he didn't need her help. At least, any more of it. But this was the first time her opinion on a business matter had been consciously solicited.

Her opinion. Not her anonymous male pseudonym. Directly solicited. Not like the last encounter, when Bryony had blurted out her opinions on beverage prices without being asked.

This was unprecedented. Max might not know her identity, but he knew she was a woman. He believed she had a brain. And possessed an opinion that only a fool would fail to listen to.

She opened the journal to the first page. "What is this?"

"Daily profit by table," he responded at once. "The key at the bottom indicates which game is played at which table, and the index at the back lists any dates in which a dedicated table changed from one game to another."

Bryony warmed at his words.

What he did not say was, *it may be too difficult for you to keep the legend straight.*

Nor did he say, *it will be impossible for you to hold the changes in dates in your memory as you sort through the daily profit records.*

Perhaps he thought she could do it. Perhaps he did not. Either way, he took care not to presume. He simply offered her the opportunity to try.

She scanned the legend first. The fluttering did not leave her chest.

The journal was a work in progress. There was no way to sort and edit information after the fact, other than to completely rewrite the entire thing. This might be how she would have attacked the problem, too.

Twenty tables, numbered in order of purchase. Once the table numbers were fixed in her mind, she flipped to the rear of the journal for the index of dates.

It was not as difficult to track the numbers as she might have thought. Some tables by necessity were designed to do one thing, such as Faro, but other tables had changed from one game to another depending on its waxing or waning popularity at any given time.

She flipped through the pages of the book as fast as she could to get a sense of its composition.

Daily reports by table were summed at end of week, summed again at end of month, then summed again at end of year.

The daily report was the only place that showed

all the numbers in full detail.

"I don't know," she said honestly as she handed back the journal.

He raised his brows. "It's impossible to say?"

"It's impossible to say at a glance," she clarified. "You need to refine the numbers."

He leaned back. "How so?"

"It would be helpful to know what a given table or game earns per hour," she explained. "Perhaps time of day is a factor. It could be that whist tables are more popular in the afternoon, and casino by night. If that is the case, it could be more profitable to designate early games and late games rather than add additional tables that sit vacant part of every day."

"But if you had to guess?" he pressed.

"Hazard, I suppose." She grinned at him shyly. "Even at a glance I can see that game garners more players at higher bids, which implies a higher percentage to the house. But I would still do the other calculations to be certain."

Max inclined his head. "I rather think you would."

She was itching to do so, in fact. He kept a tantalizing puzzle in the volume of his journals.

All the necessary observations were right there. With enough time, she could tell him at what hour of what day which games reached peak profitability. Whether their position in the salon had a factor. Was

it better to be closer to the bar? Or further from pry-
ing eyes?

What about the number of people at each table?
Some games could only be played with a certain
number of participants, but others were more flexi-
ble. Did an artificial cap create a false sense that one
was more likely to win, thus encouraging riskier
bids? Or did a greater number of competitors increase the pot on its own, encouraging higher and
higher bids?

The answers were right there in his journal, waiting to be discovered. Her blood hummed at all the
untapped potential. If this were her club...

But of course it wasn't. She might own the deed
to the property, but in a few weeks' time, their original investment contract would come to an end.

Max would owe her nothing. No money, no
monthly reports. Not even his time.

She could either content herself with receiving
rents without knowing any other detail, or she could
sell him the property outright as he so desperately
wished for her to do.

In either case, she would soon belong even less
than she did now.

She shifted uncomfortably on her perch on the
edge of his desk.

Max glanced up at her. "New trousers?"

"Old trousers," she said without thinking.

He tilted his head. "They're different from last

time."

Her heart fluttered. "You've been keeping an eye on my trousers?"

He gave her a slow, devastating smile. "I've definitely been keeping an eye on your... trousers."

Her cheeks heated in pleasure. Perhaps extravagant gowns weren't so important after all. "They're my brother's trousers. Or at least, they were."

"Does he know you took them?" he asked.

She nodded. "He gave them to me."

He raised his brows. "I would like to meet your brother."

You already have.

Bryony wondered what Max would think if he ever realized that Heath Grenville, fixer of all of Society's scandals, had willingly loaned men's clothing to not one but two of his sisters.

"Have you any siblings?" Bryony asked instead.

He hesitated. "A sister."

"I should like to meet her," she blurted. Any sister of Max's must be equally fascinating.

"No," he said curtly and turned back to his journals.

Bryony could not help but feel that she had just received the cut direct.

It was embarrassing to think she was not good enough to meet the sister of a man who ran a gambling club, but nor could she blame him for being selective. Just because he tolerated her here did not mean he wished to spend additional time in her company. She glanced away.

What did he see when he looked at her? Neither man nor a woman, perhaps. An unwanted distraction.

He did not kick her out of his office, but nor had he ever invited her to return. She was supposed to be smart. Perhaps that was her clue.

What if he didn't want her here at all, but was simply too much of a gentleman to demand that she leave, now that he knew she was a lady? Her heart twisted.

The Cloven Hoof had quickly become one of her favorite refuges. Yet perhaps all she was doing was ruining Max's solitude. If she never came back, would he even notice her absence? Would he be grateful that she had finally taken the hint?

A shiver of mortification slid down her spine and she gave herself an involuntary hug for warmth. Foolish girl. She should leave. This had gone on long enough.

As if reading her mind, Max leapt to his feet.

Bryony slid from his desk in embarrassment. "I'm going to—"

"I've got it," he interrupted, and walked past her to the fireplace, where he reached for a fire iron to stoke the flames higher.

Her heart skipped in wonder.

He had not registered her awkwardness, but

sensed her shiver. He was not afraid she would stay, but worried she might go.

Speechless at this new development, she stepped closer to him just as he turned to face her. Their feet tangled.

He caught her before she could crash into him, but did not immediately let her go.

Possibly because she held onto him for dear life.

The fireiron clanged forgotten to the carpet. They both ignored it. Their eyes were on each other.

There were no protective layers of shift and gown and lace separating her legs from his.

His powerful thighs were encased in skintight buckskin, soft leather over hard muscles just inviting to be touched.

Her own legs trembled in thin nankeen trousers, her hips inches from his.

Because the club was not yet open, she had tossed her greatcoat on the settee where it too could afford her no protection. Her brother's old jacket was too tight to button over her bosom, so she hadn't bothered. Which left her with little between them.

The thin linen shirt might hide her chest from view, but Bryony suspected Max could sense the heaving of her lungs and the frantic beating of her heart all the same.

His breath had quickened as much as hers.

Was he going to kiss her? Or were they going to stand locked together like this for eternity? She wasn't sure which she desired more. The anticipation was exquisite.

He lifted a hand to her cheek and dragged the pad of his thumb over her trembling lower lip.

"Where are you right now?" he asked softly. "Are you here in the moment with me or is that brain of yours off analyzing from afar?"

She was very much here with him. Every inch of her was more aware of his body and his presence than anything she'd ever experienced. His mouth was so close. She had not been calculating or analyzing their situation until he mentioned it, but now that he did...

Blast her luck.

Bryony swallowed. As much as she wanted him to kiss her, she could not let him do so. He would have no interest in trading kisses with the investor who refused to sell him his property. The moment would be ruined.

Worse, she liked him too much to allow her first kiss to be under false pretenses. She didn't want him to be smitten by some mystery persona that didn't truly exist. She wanted him to see her as *Bryony*.

Her skin pricked with nervousness. She had kept her secrets for long enough. Come what may, she would not go another moment before telling the truth. She respected Max too much to keep him in the dark.

When he kissed her, if he ever did kiss her, she

wanted it to be because he was truly choosing *her*.

Chapter 9

*M*ax was frozen in time and place. He hadn't meant to touch her. Had been trying as hard as humanly possible to keep his eyes on his sums and not on the rosy plumpness of her lips, just begging to be kissed.

Struggling to keep his hands busied safely atop his desk and not buried deep in her hair. Or curved about her cheek so he could stroke her lower lip as he was doing now.

This was a mistake. An aberration. He devised plans and he stuck to the plan, and in no version of any of his plans was he pulling a strange woman into his arms in the back of his office before he'd secured the Cloven Hoof as fully his own.

But Bryony didn't seem like a stranger. Or rather, he liked all the ways that she was strange.

She was smart, quick. She could sum columns in her head, backward and upside-down, but it was more than that. Her strong opinions were not meant to show off, but to improve the Cloven Hoof's profitability and efficiency.

Some men might not find a shared affinity for one's gambling den as romantic as Max, but of course those men's entire future was not wrapped up in the success or failure of a single venture. A month ago, Bryony hadn't known him, and yet her gut reaction was to help whenever possible. Because she cared.

Her ideas were sound and selfless. Her pockets did not depend on the price of his imported wines. How refreshing was that?

He still didn't know what twist of fate had caused her to sneak into his establishment that first night, but he had looked forward to each visit ever since.

Here was an intelligent woman who chose to seek out his company time and again. Her genteel accent indicated her birth was higher than his, but Max wasn't proposing marriage.

Indeed, he had vowed not to start a romance of any kind until he finally owned the deed and was able to turn the Cloven Hoof into twice the success that it already was, ensuring a stable future for his sister, himself, and his eventual wife.

That much hadn't changed. But there was a vast difference between a romantic entanglement and a simple kiss, was there not?

What harm could come of lowering his mouth to Bryony's just this once? She was so open, so honest. And he yearned to taste her lips.

One kiss. Nothing more. One kiss, and that would be the end. They would put out this impossible spark between them. One kiss, nothing more.

He stroked her cheek, hoping she could not see the battle within. He needed to concentrate on his business. Not on women. Not even on her. He could not risk allowing himself to be vulnerable.

And yet the harder he tried to push her from his mind, the more she filled his every waking thought. Now here she was, in his arms. Gazing up at him. Waiting for him to kiss her.

There was no sense fighting Fate.

He lowered his head until their breath mingled, giving her every opportunity to push away... Or pull him close.

"I'm the investor," she blurted out just before his lips grazed hers.

Max jerked his head backwards. "What?"

"The investor. I am Basil Q. Jones. Your investor." Her cheeks were bright red.

"My investor?" Max repeated blankly.

"And landlord," she continued with a grimace. "I suppose that's the most pressing of the issues. I did receive your offer. I'm considering it."

"Landlord?" Max frowned, his thoughts spinning.

"I meant to tell you." She winced and shook her head. "Actually, no, I was never going to tell you. But then I liked you, and I thought you liked me, and then I wanted to kiss you, and when I thought you were going to kiss me... I couldn't not tell you. You needed to know who you would be kissing."

"I was going to kiss Basil Q. Jones?" His stomach bottomed. She was not who he thought she was after all. She had tricked him.

Bryony nodded. "Exactly. I'm sorry. Not about being Basil, but about finding out like this. If it's all the same to you, I would very much like to continue both relationships. Business and personal."

The pieces clicked into place with horrifying precision. "You invested in my business under an assumed name, purchased the property we stand on out from under me despite my invested interest, donned a male costume in order to disguise your identity and trespass in my office—"

"Not trespassing," she pointed out with an embarrassed flash of a smile. "Landlord, remember? I own this place."

"It is *not* all the same to me," Max bit out in fury. He stalked past her and flung open the office door before he could say something they both would regret. "Get out."

"You do realize," she began.

"I *do* realize," he agreed. "Now, anyway. You have never been honest with me, not once. Not the disguise, not your name, not even your reason for being here."

"I never meant to meet you," she said in a rush. "I knew you were closed on Tuesdays, which is why I chose that day to—"

"Legally but unethically enter this building to rifle through my private belongings," he finished, his disgust in her rivaled only by his disgust in himself. He had allowed himself to be deceived because he had wanted to believe she was different.

"It sounds bad," she admitted.

"It is bad," he corrected, keeping his voice as cold and businesslike as possible. There was nothing else between them. Not now. "The subterfuge was unnecessary. I send you monthly reports. If there was anything else you needed to know—"

Max's fingers shook. She hadn't been trying to discover his club's weaknesses. She'd been looking for *his*. And she'd found them.

A harsh laugh escaped his throat as he replayed their various encounters in his mind.

Her cheeks paled.

"Were you laughing on the inside when I handed you my journals?" Of course she was. "No wonder it was easy for you to make quick judgments. You had seen all the details before. Knew my business as well as I did before you even walked in the door."

She bit her lip. "It wasn't like that. I mean, yes, I have committed all of your monthly reports to memory. But that isn't why I'm here. My suggestions for improvement and future opportunities for analysis were both spontaneous and sincere."

"Sincerely trying to line your own pockets," he said flatly.

She winced. "Our contract is up in a little over a month. You won't owe me a percentage after that."

"But you will still own the deed." The completed contract was immaterial. Keeping him beholden was where the money was. He could do sums as well as she could. "That's why you're here, isn't it? To learn how much you can squeeze from me in rents before I break?"

"No," she hedged. "Although, objectively speaking, that would be the wisest business decision in this circumstance."

He glared at her.

"I said no," she said quickly. "And I meant it. I did sneak in to see what I could learn that you weren't telling me. You're right about that. But it was never my intention to treat you unfairly."

"Wasn't it?" He advanced on her, his cold voice sharp enough to cut glass. "You were just going to *fairly* sneak into my office when you knew that I was away, and *fairly* snoop through my journals and any other private documentation you could find, in order to *fairly* respond to an offer that is already double any reasonable market value?"

Her lip trembled. She looked miserable.

He didn't care.

"Please don't push me away," she begged. "We did not meet under the best of circumstances, I admit. What I witnessed the first night showed me who you truly were. I didn't return because of my investment in the Cloven Hoof. The reason I keep coming back... is you."

"I can't push you away," he reminded her, his voice cold. "You own the deed and a stake in my business. But what I can do is ask you politely to get the bloody hell out of my sight."

She flinched.

At first, he thought she would run.

He should've known better. She wasn't the sort to back down from danger—or confrontation.

"I do own the deed and a temporary stake in the business," she agreed, her eyes flashing. "I came here to see if selling the land to you was the proper decision, and I have not yet made up my mind. That I have enjoyed our time together does not signify. I will not make a decision on the sale of the deed until our contract is through. If you want to influence the outcome, you will allow me to shadow you here until I've made my decision."

"And if I say no?" he growled.

She lifted her chin. "Then I guess we have nothing left to discuss."

Meaning if he kept her out of his club... She would keep the property out of spite. Untenable.

Nor was he willing to let her toy with him on a string for a month and still not sell him the property at the end of the contract.

He crossed his arms. "I will agree to tolerate your presence until our contract is through if you put into writing that you will absolutely sell me the property at a to-be-determined price."

"No deal," she said and turned toward the door.

He grabbed her wrist and spun her to face him. "Damn it, woman."

The shadowed look in her brown eyes was closer to sorrow than victory.

"One month," she said softly. "I'll put in writing that I will give you a final answer at the end of the month, but I cannot yet commit to what that answer will be."

He dropped her arm in disgust and turned his back in her direction. "Be careful out there, Basil. Some unsavory character may rob you blind."

Chapter 10

*M*ax glared across his small dining room table at his sister.

"She does not sound like an interesting woman," he corrected Frances firmly. "She sounds like a holy terror. A viper, waiting for her chance to strike. One part Medusa, one part siren."

"Great voice, bad hair?" Frances asked innocently, clearly trying not to laugh. "Please clarify in what sense you mean the metaphor about turning hard as stone when you see her?"

"I meant in the 'dangerous woman' sense," he growled, ignoring her ribald jest. "The sort of woman who drives men to their deaths. Ruins their lives."

This time, Frances did laugh. "You have never met your match, much less a woman capable of besting you. Either you are exaggerating, dear brother, or she is exactly what you need."

"She lied to me," he said flatly.

"Lies are bad," Frances agreed. "Would you have let her in to your club if she'd been completely honest from the start?"

Max snorted. "Of course not."

"Well, there you go." Frances spooned a lump of sugar into her tea.

He stared at her. "Your argument is that all deception is rendered immaterial if the owner of a gentleman's club finds himself in the obvious predicament of not wanting to allow a *woman* into his *gentleman's club*?"

Frances lifted her tea to her lips. "Yes."

"You are no help," he told her. "You are worse than no help."

"Did you want help?" She arched a brow. "I never thought you needed help."

He ignored her. "Change the subject. Let me see the new waistcoat."

Her eyes narrowed. "You say that as if there were some approval process through which your new garments must pass. I sewed them, you will wear them. Non-negotiable."

"Let me see them," he repeated.

"Why did you want them?" Frances asked instead.

"No reason," Max said quickly. "Keep them. I don't need them."

"Ohhh, for *her*," his sister sing-songed in the most irritating manner possible.

"Not for her," Max insisted. "I just happened to be in the haberdasher—"

"As one does," Frances interrupted. "Especially when one lives on the opposite side of town and possesses no affinity toward fashion."

"—admiring the rows of fabric—"

"As one does," Frances murmured again. "Especially when one is the owner of a gaming hell famous for being swathed in shadow and darkness."

"—and the haberdasher talked me into it against my will," Max concluded.

"No one has ever talked you into anything in all your life," Frances pointed out with a knowing look. "You bought waistcoats because you meant to, and you *let* Bryony into your life. You rolled the dice."

Max shook his head. "I thought she was someone else."

"False." Frances sipped her tea. "You had absolutely no idea who she was."

"I certainly didn't think she owned the land and property housing my club."

"Because she's a woman?" Frances asked. "And women can't own things?"

Max ignored this. "And I certainly didn't think she would use the deed as leverage to manipulate me into dancing to her tune."

"Because she's a woman?" Frances asked again.

"And women cannot be as merciless, cunning, and ruthless as men?"

"Ha! So you admit she is merciless, cunning, and ruthless." Max crossed his arms in satisfaction. "You see why I cannot like her."

She gave an unladylike shrug. "It seems like you have a lot in common."

His heart thumped, aghast. "You are not trying to matchmake, are you? Why is everyone trying to matchmake me?"

Frances selected a biscuit. "Where there's smoke, there's hellfire. You did meet at the Cloven Hoof."

"She's mercenary," he reminded her. "She tried to profit off of me."

"She is successfully profiting off of you," Frances pointed out. "And you, her. Your club would not exist if she had not taken a chance when no one else would."

"And it will never be what I need it to be if I cannot own my property," he said with a frustrated sigh.

His sister's calculating expression turned serious. "You didn't tell me it was personal."

"The Cloven Hoof is our future, Fran." He let out a deep breath. "At least, it was meant to be. Every shilling I've earned is now tied up in a connected investment that will only bear fruit if I can get my hands on the deed."

Frances considered his words. "Can you steal it?"

"Out of the question," he said flatly.

"Can you marry her for it?"

He nearly laughed. "Even further out of the question."

"Have you offered enough money for it?" she asked.

"More than twice what it's worth, and still she toys with me."

Frances raised her eyebrows. "What exactly did she say?"

He ground his teeth. "That she would give me a final decision at the end of a month's time, and not a moment before."

"A month of learning more about the business in order to make an informed decision about how best her money should be spent?" his sister asked adroitly.

He slanted her a look. "Frances—"

"All I'm saying," she interrupted, "is that it doesn't seem like she's toying with you. You may not like her actions or her choices, but she's given you a deadline and an explanation that make sense. You just don't like being on the receiving end of someone else's grand scheme."

"Who does?" he asked darkly.

Frances reached for another biscuit.

She deserved so much more. So much better. Max wished he had been there for her from the beginning.

The day she had gained employment as a maid-of-all-work, they'd known it would be grueling hours for very little pay, but at least she would be safe and warm and dry and fed.

Except, the master of the house tried to make her into his whore. When she'd fled, sobbing, arriving on Max's doorstep with no references and no self-respect, believing she had somehow brought the assault on herself, Max had lost control.

He flew straight to the home of the supposed "gentleman" and demanded an audience. When he was not granted one, he muscled his way inside and demanded to meet at dawn in order to defend his sister's honor with a loaded pistol.

Her employer had laughed in Max's face. Dueling was a gentleman's privilege, not a dockworker's. There were no charges that would stick. Not with the word of a slut against her master. The so-called gentleman immediately had Max thrown out on his ear and reported to the constable for nuisance.

By then, their mother was too ill to work. Max swore on her deathbed that he would protect his sister from such monsters in the future, and swore to himself to enact revenge on one cruel bastard in particular.

That he suspected Bryony to be of the same world—a world that considered people like his family, like his sister, to be as inferior as insects—was a detail he had refrained from sharing with Frances.

He much preferred to see her smiling and teasing than for her to think they were once again being trod beneath the heel of someone else's boot.

A sharp knock rapped upon the door.

Max and his sister met eyes in surprise. She was the only visitor he had ever had. No one else had any clue where he lived.

Perhaps it was a lost traveler. Or a neighbor.

He rose from the table and went to answer the door.

A well-dressed footman held out a folded missive, sealed with expensive wax.

"Mr. Gideon?"

Max accepted the letter in silence.

The elegant footman immediately vanished back to his master.

"Who is it?" Frances called. "Is something amiss?"

"I don't know."

He broke the seal and unfolded the letter.

Meet me at the row of trees opposite Gunter's. We need to talk.
Basil

Max crumpled up the paper and hurled it across the room into the fire.

"That looked like good paper," his sister protested. "We could have used it for something."

"I'd rather be warm," he growled. Just seeing her handwriting gave him shivers.

Frances's eyes lit up. "Was it her?"

"Indeed," he agreed with a sour voice. "She sent for me like a servant."

Frances tilted her head. "Sent you where?"

"Gunter's ices," Max admitted grudgingly.

Frances immediately reached for the new waistcoats. "Wear the green one."

Max shook his head. A dragon's underbelly was too vulnerable. With Bryony, he would need to be strong. As sudden and unpredictable as a thunderstorm. "I'll wear the blue."

As soon as he was straightened and buttoned and coiffed, Frances all but pushed him out the door.

"Tell her I want to meet her," she called as he flagged down a hackney.

"Never," he called back as he climbed inside.

The drive to Gunter's only gave him more time to fume.

He didn't know Bryony's surname, and she knew everything about him. Even his home direction. The power imbalance was entirely in her favor and he didn't like it one bit.

When the hack let him out, it took a moment to espy her amongst all the fashionable folk lining the street outside.

He had become so used to seeing her in shirt-sleeves and trousers that at first he forgot to even look at the fine ladies in flamboyant bonnets and expensive walking gowns.

When their gazes met, Bryony's eyes laughed at him as if she had anticipated his confusion.

That wasn't all he felt.

Her long, slender legs were hidden beneath the frothy folds of a buttery yellow gown. Her bosom, unfettered by bindings, was highlighted by a jaunty band of glass and sequins that dazzled as it caught the sunlight. Her hair was not hidden beneath a crooked beaver hat, but piled atop her head in a profusion of artfully placed curls that made her look like a goddess.

Or Medusa.

He stalked over to her. "Where is your chaperone?"

She gestured over her shoulder at a maid far more interested in consuming flavored ices than paying any attention to her mistress.

"First things first." Bryony gestured to two heaping bowls on a small stool. "I didn't know which flavor you might like, so I chose the two most popular in the hopes that one would do. Do you prefer jasmine or violet?"

"Neither," he growled. His stomach gurgled in protest. "Why did you summon me here?"

"It's a beautiful day." She lifted a hand toward

the unseasonably clear sky. "I thought we should meet somewhere neutral. Not the Cloven Hoof."

"Why?" he repeated.

"I wanted you to meet me as me," she said after a long moment, as she played with one of her ringlets. "And perhaps share an ice or two."

"We are not friends," he reminded her. "I'm not your suitor or even a willing business partner."

She stopped toying with her artful tendrils to frown at him. "You could be a willing business partner if you wished."

He stared back at her without responding.

"And we could be friends," she continued softly, hesitantly. "If you wanted to."

He chose one of the bowls of slowly melting ice and handed her the other.

"Eat this," he said gruffly. "And stop playing with your hair. It looks like it took an hour to curl."

"Two," Bryony muttered. "It apparently takes longer if you fidget."

He frowned. "Why bother if you dislike it?"

"This is one of the first times I *have* bothered," she admitted.

Max shoved a spoonful of flavored ice in his mouth before he could inquire whether she'd done so for him. Because she wanted him to find her beautiful. As if he didn't already.

"I like your waistcoat," she said shyly. "It reminds me of the deepest parts of the ocean.

Somewhere a Kraken might live."

Damn it. It was hard to stay furious at a woman whose views mirrored his.

"Bryony," squealed a trio of blonde females as they flocked over as one. "Tell your mother to send us a new invitation. Ours never arrived."

"She won't," Bryony said between spoonfuls of ice. "She's hoping to marry me off to the first man whose signature she can forge on a wedding contract, and it won't work if all the eligible gentlemen are distracted by you three."

Marry her off?

Surely the somersaults in Max's stomach were because such a turn would be disastrous news for the future of his club. When Bryony married, the deed would belong to some titled toff, not to her.

The girls giggled and pouted. "How are you supposed to charm anyone if you're playing the violin instead of conversing?"

"Mother believes that's the only time I *am* charming," Bryony said with a self-deprecating chuckle. "She'll be at Lady Roundtree's on Wednesday, if you want to press your case then."

"Your mother doesn't know everything," one of the chits assured her earnestly. "Why, just look at your hair. It *can* curl!"

The other girls chimed in with their effusive agreement.

"Thank you for noticing," Bryony said with a

straight face. "These ringlets are my greatest achievement. The culmination of four Seasons' hopes and dreams."

"They're very pretty." The girls cast curious glances at Max. "And..."

Bryony stared back at them without blinking.

After an increasingly awkward stretch of silence, they curtsied and left without a single word in his direction.

"Friendly bunch," he said when they were gone.

"Oh, were you hoping they would speak to you?" Bryony asked sweetly. "I'm afraid they couldn't do so without an introduction."

"You could have introduced them."

"And have them charm you out from under me? I think not. Especially when I haven't a violin handy with which to drown out their sweetness."

"Do you play in a theater?" he asked, curious despite himself.

She shook her head. "At home, and at my sister's school."

He had heard music at Vauxhall, but never touched an instrument of his own. "You must love it."

"I hate it," she admitted. "I often feel the only time I contribute as a respectable part of my family is when I'm on stage. And I'm always on stage."

That... was not what he'd imagined it would be like.

"Then why do you do it?"

"Because I love my family," she said simply. "Why else would I do anything? Aren't the people you love always worth it?"

Damn it. Max set down his empty bowl with more force than necessary.

It was hard to stay angry with a woman who valued her family as much as he valued his.

"What kind of high-in-the-instep school needs a violinist?" he asked instead.

Bryony's eyes shone. "A struggling boarding school in St. Giles. A few of the girls attend on paid tuition now, but most of the students are orphans or runaways my sister felt should have a better life. She gives them an education and skills with which to find gainful employment of their choice."

Max tried not to show how surprised and impressed he was. "The violin helps with that?"

"Not at all," she answered with pride. "The violin is for pleasure. Music to dance by. Everyone deserves a few moments when they can truly be free."

Max glowered at her.

It sounded perfect. She sounded perfect. Yet he could tell just by looking at her to which class she belonged. He'd spent his life vowing to outwit the aristocracy, not fall for one. He would not make that mistake.

"Is your mother truly searching for a husband for you?" he asked.

"As if it were her job," Bryony answered with

feeling. "Not that Mother would ever perform something so common as a *job*. Finding me a husband is more like... her calling."

Max's stomach once again gave an uncomfortable twist.

He wasn't jealous. How could he be? He didn't want Bryony for himself. Couldn't have her, even if he did. Even if she weren't from her class, even if he wasn't from his, even if they'd both been born in the same rookery, romance still wouldn't be an option.

She held the deed to his property *and* the upper hand.

He had to find a way to convince her to sell. And not using one of his sister's harebrained ideas.

If it were even possible to marry Bryony, that would be cheating in the worst way. One must earn one's success. He intended to be a self-made man before he wed, not because of it. Afterward, he would choose a wife for love, not papers, or he wouldn't take one at all.

And Bryony would choose a husband for... Who knew what criteria a woman of her class would have? Money, he supposed. A title, no doubt. Looks, status, social connections. They couldn't be more different. She was beauty and he was the beast.

He preferred being the beast.

It helped remind him that the only reason Bryony could be interested in him outside of the Cloven Hoof was because to her he was exotic and different.

A way to be rebellious. A momentary diversion for now, and immaterial in the future.

In a few months, when she became Lady Whatever, the growing business he'd spent blood, sweat, and his life savings building from nothing would merely be an amusing anecdote she might share with her friends as they sipped champagne at some Society ball.

He didn't care about her world. He had a world of his own, a world that didn't include her. His club, his friends, his sister... Bryony didn't fit any part of it. It was good for both of them to remember that.

"You're scowling again," she told him. "I presume I've managed to vex you in some new and unpredictable way."

His eyes narrowed. "I was just thinking how grateful I am that I'll never be forced to marry a spoiled rich girl."

"Good one," she said approvingly. "An arrow right to my spoiled rich parts." She lowered her voice. "That's all of me, in case you were wondering."

He burst out laughing without meaning to.

She was impossible to offend. She didn't take herself seriously enough. Her friends sounded tolerable, her mother sounded awful, and he himself wasn't exactly known as someone who was easy to get along with.

Except she made it easy. She saw him for who

and what he was and didn't appear to mind. If anything, she seemed to prefer him exactly how he was. She didn't judge him. She didn't care enough about what anyone else thought to bother. He could be open and honest with her in a manner that he could never replicate with the patrons of his club.

Damn it, he *liked* her.

"There you are," shrilled a voice. "Esther, go ask Miss Grenville why you haven't received an invitation to the family musicale. She's standing right there."

Max jerked his gaze toward Bryony.

Miss Grenville.

Violin.

Musicale.

Basil Q. Jones was Heath Grenville's sister. His *business associate* Heath Grenville, secret-keeper for the *ton* and solver of problems, including the conundrum of how to raise startup funds for an unusual gambling club. Not to mention heir apparent to a barony.

Bryony's parents were *titled*. She didn't just have a subscription to Almack's. She was a member of the aristocracy. Sharing ices in the park was madness. His very presence could ruin her reputation, if he were recognized. Her father could hogtie him on a boat to Australia for such presumption.

As a lord, he would face no repercussion for the crime. Just sympathy from his peers.

Bryony knew this. Had known it all along and didn't care.

She was too busy making some sort of statement in front of her friends. The dashing, rebellious hoyden who had brought a king of the underworld to heel. She hadn't brought him here to discuss selling him the deed to his property. She had put him on display like a dog.

Max took a step backwards.

She glanced over at him sharply. "All the countless ways that I've been horrid to you, and you retreat when you discover I'm a Grenville?"

"I'm not your plaything," he said. "And I'm not your gewgaw, to be gawked at by your fancy friends."

She stepped forward, eyes startled. "That's not what—"

"I'll see you back at the office, Miss Grenville. Until then, don't call."

He tipped his hat to the onlookers and walked away.

Chapter 11

*F*rom her position hidden behind the folding screen separating the settee from the rest of the office, Bryony had begun to feel like an all-knowing but impotent ghost.

After Max had discovered the truth of who she was, Bryony had been afraid her status as daughter of a baron and all that entailed would cause him to shut her out. According to Society, she should have nothing to do with him, nor he with her—under any circumstances.

Then again, according to Society, a gambling den like Max's should not exist, much less be as wildly popular as it was. To Bryony, the attraction of the Cloven Hoof was less the income it could raise and more the escape it could provide.

Indeed, she could not help but wonder if that was

the reason so many gamblers of different backgrounds risked their livelihoods within its walls. A
chance to escape from reality.

Perhaps she had overestimated the allure of an
easy monetary windfall and underestimated the irresistible draw being somewhere absolutely nothing
was expected of you.

"Thank you so much," said the fourth person that
evening.

Bryony knew because she had been transcribing
each conversation into her journal. She couldn't see
who the man might be, but each word was clear.

"Remember," Max told his visitor sternly. "No
more horses."

He had taken Bryony very much at her word. She
intended to shadow his office for the next month? So
be it. The Cloven Hoof had many shadows.

She was relegated posthaste to the corner behind
the folding screen, and completely forgotten.

Ever since that day at Gunter's, she'd spent more
hours of each night on this settee than in her own
bedchamber, to mixed results. She knew the Cloven
Hoof and its clientele more intimately than ever. But
her relationship with its arrogant, fiercely independent owner was icy at best.

"Are you too busy to interrupt?" queried a nervous male voice.

"Not for you," came Max's immediate reply.

Bryony's hidden smile was brittle.

He was angry with her for forcing him to make a compromise not of his choosing.

She hadn't wished to hold the property deed over his head like blackmail, but she had been desperate. He had backed her into a corner from which she saw no other escape. She could not bear to lose him from her life so soon after finding him.

A month from now, her parents could have her betrothed and headed a hundred miles away. But between then and now, she wanted to spend as much time at the Cloven Hoof as possible.

It was the closest she had ever come to feeling like she was somewhere she belonged.

"—and ever since, the Queen of Diamonds has been my lucky card," explained the current guest.

"When gambling one's unentailed home," Max said with considerable patience, "there is no such thing as a lucky card."

Bryony grinned at the folding screen.

It would be easier if she could dislike him. If he truly were the demon Society painted him to be. But she had seen the truth. She gazed at him through the crack beside the folding screen.

He was the angel of the underworld. A granter of miracles. A giver of hope, to those most in need.

One could not help but admire him.

"Have you considered my offer?" came a new voice, crackling with hope.

"I have," Max responded. "I shall invest at ten

percent."

Her heart gave a little flutter. Everything she'd wished she could be doing when she used her anonymous accounts to transfer funds out of her savings and into lives where it would make more of an impact, Max did every day. Without pseudonyms. Without secrecy. Without shame. He was able to openly help others and receive much-deserved credit for all of his accomplishments.

Women like Bryony would never be able to do the same.

To be sure, she would soon be praised on the fine catch her parents managed to scrounge for her. It would be a lie. Her elder sister was sweet, biddable, and beautiful, and the suitor their parents had procured for poor Camellia was a man twice her age from the other side of England. So far away, the sisters had feared they would lose contact altogether.

Bryony's fortune would be far worse than that. Her strongest qualities weren't the sort that anyone admired.

Except for Max.

As angry as he'd been with her for manipulating him, he was no fool. He was a pragmatist. Once the deal was struck, he'd immediately put her to work. She was not behind the settee twiddling fingers as she eavesdropped. She was sharing the settee with a stack of old journals, a pile of new pencils, and a fresh journal in which to analyze, calculate, and conclude for Max's benefit.

"What if he doesn't pay his vowels?" came a tremulous voice on the other side of the folding screen. "I cannot take him to the courts. If the House of Lords won't convict murder, they certainly won't side with a humble shopkeeper over a marquess."

"I don't need the House of Lords at my disposal in order to ruin him." Max's voice was calm. Simply stating facts. "Tell him he has a fortnight or he's answerable to me."

Bryony's stomach flipped. He was as brilliant as he was ruthless. Driven to succeed at any cost. She could not have respected him more.

If she were forced to come up with something she disliked about Maxwell Gideon, it would be that he was able to perform his amazing feats and defy every odd, while she was powerless to even try.

Proper ladies did not run businesses of any kind. They were too busy running their husbands' household. Any assets they possessed prior to the marriage were forfeit the day of the wedding. The husband's word was now law. The wife's role, to provide him with children. Sons. Someone who could inherit and be important. Someone capable of starting a legacy of his own.

It was enough to make a woman scream.

"Closing time," came the low, familiar rumble of Max's voice. "We are alone."

A delicious shiver raced down Bryony's spine.

Ever since that one electrically charged moment when he had almost kissed her, Max had not tried again. Perhaps he no longer wished to.

Bryony did not feel the same.

When she did not immediately leap out from her hiding place to address him, Max's footsteps stalked closer. With the swipe of one powerful arm, he shoved the offending folding screen out of the way and glared down at her for daring to disobey his unspoken wishes.

She grinned up at him. This was part of their routine. She was not the sort who obeyed, and he was the sort to act.

For the first time tonight, the intense focus of that dark glittering gaze was finally all hers. There were no more distractions. Just the two of them, and the live sparks crackling between.

"You were very sweet tonight," she said to annoy him. "I love how benevolent you are to those who have nowhere else to turn. A soft heart is commendable."

He was not amused. "You've read the journals. I make a tidy profit from my so-called benevolence."

"Of course you do," Bryony agreed. "How else would you continue to be the secret benefactor of the underworld?"

He folded his arms over his chest. "I could use the money earned from gaming tables."

"No doubt you will." Bryony considered the idea.

"You're in a much better position to distribute their excess spoils where it ought to go than any of those featherwits."

Max turned and walked over to his desk without replying.

She smiled.

He knew her as well as she knew him. Of course she would follow close behind in order to take her customary place perched on the corner of his desk. She brought the journals with her.

Mining their secrets had become something of an obsession. This might be her last opportunity to make herself useful in a situation such as this.

Max might not have explicitly asked for her help, but he had given her the journals. Trusted her with their contents. Trusted her conclusions.

Max, who trusted no one.

Except Bryony.

Some of her happy warmth faded. If only he *liked* her. Although he might trust her with his business, he definitely didn't trust her with his heart. She doubted he ever would.

"Are you done yet?" he asked.

"Ye of little faith." She placed her working journal on the desk in front of him. "I finished the first project yesterday. Indexes A and B explain the variables charting profit relationships between game and table, as promised. I have moved on to more complex functions including position in the salon as well as time and day."

This was exactly the sort of talk her mother had all but tried to beat out of her in desperation. No one liked a female who thought herself clever. How was she ever going to attract a man?

"Your impertinence is your second-best quality," Max muttered as he accepted the journal and perused her handiwork.

She raised her brows in interest. "What is my best quality?"

He gestured without looking up from the charts she painstakingly created for him. "How your arse looks in trousers."

Bryony's pulse leaped. He *did* find her attractive. Had carnal thoughts when he looked at her, just as she did when she thought of him. An excited shiver went up her spine.

Perhaps he hadn't stopped being angry with her. But nor had he ceased being aware of her in all the same ways she was constantly aware of him. He hadn't forgotten that almost kiss either.

And he liked how she looked in trousers. Her heart soared.

He flipped back and forth between two of the pages. "These charts are almost identical."

Pulse still racing, she pulled her chair around to his side. "It surprised me as well. But when one plots the income the day before the Cloven Hoof closes for twenty-four hours, compared to Wednesdays when we reopen—"

Heads nearly touching, they spent the next hour inspecting and arguing every data point and conclusion. It was heaven. Debating with Max over the applications of raw mathematics in the context of real-world psychology were the most thrilling conversations Bryony had ever had. She cherished these moments more than any other.

There was no artifice between them. This was her. The things she thought. How she was. He pushed her, challenged her, but never tried to change her. He might never say so, but she suspected these had also become his favorite moments of the day.

Night, rather.

She pulled out her pocketwatch and made a face at the late hour. Time had run away with them again. She needed to hurry home.

She glanced over at Max just in time to see disappointment flicker across his face. Just as quickly, he wiped all emotion away until he was once more a blank mass of arrogance.

But she had seen behind the façade. He liked her arse. Perhaps he liked the rest of her, too.

"Tomorrow?" she asked softly.

He lifted one of his wide shoulders in a laconic shrug. "If you won't be too busy waltzing with future suitors."

Her heart jumped. Was that what he imagined her doing whenever she was not in his sight? He was not far off the mark, but had no reason to be jealous. None of those gentlemen were half as magnetic as he.

"I would rather be dancing with you," she whispered. She didn't mean to. The words just tumbled out.

It was the wrong thing to say.

His face shuttered immediately and he pushed to his feet. "That is unfortunate. I will never be at any of those gatherings, nor do I wish to be. Enjoy your soirées. I have better things to do with my time."

She nodded dumbly, despite the stinging in her throat. Without a word, she allowed him to walk her from the office to the exit. Their night was over. Before she slipped off in search of a hack to take her home, she turned to face him one last time.

As always, his dark eyes were unreadable.

"I meant it. I would rather be right here with you." She let her fingers brush against his a second too long before darting around the corner without giving him a chance to say he did not feel the same.

Chapter 12

*M*ax burst out of his empty apartment. The best thing about Tuesday used to be the break from the Cloven Hoof. A respite from responsibilities, twenty-four hours without accounts to pay, or reports to write. A break from other people.

But Max didn't want a break. Not from one person in particular. The one who vexed him and invigorated him and drove him mad with frustration, and longing, and impossibility.

He missed her.

No worse foolishness had ever occurred in a heart he had long kept guarded behind layers of steel and stone. He couldn't have her. Shouldn't want her. Would be rid of her in less than a month's time. A fact he should be celebrating, not mourning.

And yet here he was, dodging mud puddles on the uneven dirt street outside his home, to pay an errand boy to deliver a message to the fashionable part of town.

A missive containing only five words:

Basil,

My house.

Your devil

He gave the lad an extra shilling to ensure he would run off with haste before Max could change his mind.

Normally, Max never changed his mind. That's what planning was for.

One considered the facts. Catalogued the details. Parsed the opportunities. Once one had determined the best strategy to take, one took it. That's how he had run his entire life. The reason why he was successful.

But proper planning did not explain standing in the rain to pay an errand boy to send a very foolish message.

Irritated with himself, he turned around and strode back up the walk into his home.

He had analyzed with care. The facts were obvious. No good could come of this. She knew it; he knew it. And yet her words haunted him.

I would rather be with you.

He was not ready to admit he wished the same thing. She had tricked him, and he had not yet forgiven her. Despite his anger and disappointment, he had no choice but to acknowledge how much he missed her. It had been twelve hours. Who missed someone after twelve hours? It was ridiculous. The superlative fancy of romantic poets, not practical men who knew better.

And yet he paced from door to sitting room and back again. What if she didn't come?

What if she did?

He glanced about his small flat. There was nothing to tidy. He had never liked leaving anything not as expected. His world was ordered. Everything in its place.

Everything except a heart that seemed to be trying to beat its way out of his chest.

His invitation was not for a romantic assignation, he reminded himself. He was not as stupid as that, and neither was she. This was a...

Well, what was it, then?

A business meeting, he decided. She had succeeded very prettily in taking advantage of him, and he would do the same to her. As simple as that.

He would not touch her. That much he knew for

sure. She was the daughter of a lord, destined for the sort of gentleman who possessed a handful of courtesy titles behind his name.

But her clever mind worked in ways other brains could not. He would show her every number, every cipher, and every journal of accounts he possessed. She would have a plethora of ideas, and no shortage of saucy commentary.

There. What could be safer? He would not ruin her future prospects by divesting her of her purity.

If that was even something she thought about half as often as he did.

"Business meeting," he muttered beneath his breath, pleading his wayward thoughts to stay on track. "Numbers. Stick to the plan."

He stalked to his narrow looking-glass and glowered at his reflection.

His sister was right. The Cloven Hoof was too full of darkness and shadow for one's choice of fabric to matter. Inky black tailcoats and smoke-gray waistcoats were perfectly acceptable in such an environment.

This was special.

Bryony had already seen one of his new waistcoats the day he met her for ices. The blue one to evoke violent storms and the unpredictability of hidden currents beneath the surface of the ocean. That day, he'd felt strong. He knew what he wanted. Life was marching right to plan.

He shrugged out of his tailcoat, shucked his familiar gray waistcoat, and reached for the green one at the rear of his armoire.

Today he was no raging storm, but a dragon nesting in his cave. Waking from a long sleep. More than capable of breathing fire. An ugly beast with sharp claws and iridescent scales covering his exposed and vulnerable underbelly.

He buttoned the waistcoat and faced the looking glass.

There it was. His armor. His shield. A thin layer of expertly sewn silk disguising the vulnerable heart hiding beneath.

It would not be enough, but it would have to do. This was all that he had.

As he shrugged his tailcoat back over his shoulders, a tentative knock rapped at the door.

He froze.

She was here.

Max was no longer certain he was ready.

He crossed his apartment and yanked open the front door as if annoyed with her for heeding his invitation. Or annoyed with himself for having sent it.

"You shouldn't have come," he growled.

Her bashful smile gripped his heart. "Then you shouldn't have invited me."

She hadn't come as Basil, but as Bryony.

Her spencer was a soft ivory the color of fresh cream. Her gown, a soft lavender. Some might think it reminiscent of a delicate, fragile flower, but Max knew better. This shade was no wilting lilac, but the sharp violet of the flavored ice they'd shared when he found out her true identity.

Her bonnet was damp from the drizzle outside, and her lustrous brown hair fell straight and strong, undisturbed by the false pretenses of curling tongs.

She had come as herself. Not a lad in trousers, nor as an aristocratic lady. She was here as Bryony. The woman who haunted his office, his dreams, and now his home.

He pulled her inside and shut the door, but could not tear his gaze away.

"I've never seen you more beautiful," he said and hated himself for it.

Already the platonic business meeting was off to a rocky start.

"You've always been the most handsome man I've ever seen," she said shyly. "Your waistcoat is gorgeous. Such deep greens evoke a mystical forest. A magical wood where only the most fearless adventurers would dare to tread."

She was perfect. He was lost. The only exploring he wished to do was the taste of her moans while he—

No. This wouldn't do at all. He spun away from her and gestured at his apartment, much of which was visible from the front door.

"This is my home," he announced. "Smaller than your dressing chamber, I'm sure."

"Mm." Her eyes twinkled. "You'll have to sneak in some time and see."

He clenched his jaw at the inadvertent reminder the only way he would ever be allowed into her private chamber was if he snuck in like a thief. "Sit."

She glanced over her shoulder. "Don't I get the tour?"

"No tour." The only room still hidden from view was his bedchamber, and he would *not* be leading her there. Having her in his sitting room was temptation enough.

He led her to the two armchairs facing a small sofa.

She did not take a seat. "Why did you invite me here?"

A thousand possible answers he could never say aloud crossed Max's mind. He settled on the reason that was supposed to be true. Maybe it even was.

"You said we needed a neutral location to speak freely," he reminded her. "There isn't one. I don't belong in your world, and you must come disguised to mine. Perhaps I do compromise. My home is my territory, but at least it is a place where we can both be ourselves."

To his horror, her eyes turned glassy and she blinked several times before responding.

"Thank you," she said quietly. "I believe that is the nicest thing anyone has ever done for me."

Damn it all.

Max had believed himself the vulnerable dragon exposing his home and his heart to the invader, when in fact the mere act of lowering the drawbridge had shattered his opponent's shields and laid her bare.

He'd had it backwards. She was the dragon, and he the slayer. He had feared her power and forgotten her vulnerability.

"I didn't mean to be nice," he said gruffly. "In part, I called you here to prove how different we are. To show you that my reality is this street, this neighborhood, this apartment. Now do you see? I have no palace, no white steed or pots of gold. All I have is my sister, a gambling den—"

"—and me," Bryony finished with a wobbly smile.

"I don't have you," he said harshly. "You'll be gone in a month, you said so yourself. You will be married to Lord Moneybreeches, living off in some—"

"I'm right here." She touched a fingertip to his chest. "Lord Moneybreeches doesn't have me yet. I'm right here with you."

It still wasn't close enough.

He pulled her to him and crushed his mouth to hers.

They couldn't go on like this. There could be no promises between them. But she was right here in his home. In his life. In his arms.

Nothing had ever felt sweeter.

Her lips were as soft as he'd imagined. The tart tongue beneath a defense mechanism to keep out those who were not worthy. She opened herself to him.

He flung her bonnet aside and released the pins from her hair. Her mane was long and lustrous, a river of shining softness. He was glad she had not curled it. He never wanted her to do anything that made her feel she wasn't being true to herself.

If she preferred top hats to bonnets, so be it.

He didn't care what she wore. He cared who she *was*. All he wanted was to keep kissing her. For the rest of the day, for the rest of the week, for the rest of the month.

Who cared about calculating numbers and keeping journals? The only figures he cared about were the two of theirs pressed close together. The only plan worth following was the one that kept her mouth beneath his.

That it couldn't last was immaterial. Nothing lasted. He learned that long ago. More importantly he had also learned to take advantage of opportunities when they arose. Moments as delicious as these were fleeting, and meant to be cherished as long as possible.

She was meant to be cherished. By someone other than him, he remembered belatedly.

The bubble of forbidden joy popped.

He would not be keeping her. The best he could

hope was to give her a memory she would not soon forget.

Chapter 13

*A*lthough this was only her first kiss, Bryony realized in a heartbeat that Max's "ice king" demeanor and melting kisses had ruined her for all other men.

His body was hard, his muscles stiff, as if fighting an uncontrollable urge to plunder far more than her mouth. His lips were firm, possessive. Demanding, freely taking what the rest of him would not.

He did not seek her submission, but her very soul. Coaxed her innermost desires to the surface with every brush of his lips, every stroke of his thumb against the side of her cheek. He treated her not as if she were an unwanted interloper, but as if she were a treasure more precious than silver. Softer than rose petals. More addictive than opium.

Heaven knew she felt the same.

Her heart pounded faster than ever. She'd been lost from the first, was losing further ground by the moment. She clutched him like a life raft rescuing her from a sea of doubt and denial. In his arms lay both safety and seduction.

In the back of her mind, the whirlpool of reality threatened to pluck her out of his embrace and pull her down into the depths of despair where moments like these were forbidden and wrong.

If she were honest, she had believed giving into her desires would prove their incompatibility. That he was not for her. That together they were nothing.

Instead, everything about him was horribly, perfectly, right.

She ran her hands over his chest and secretly thrilled that he permitted her to do so. As if his body was no longer his to defend, but hers to explore. To enjoy.

His ardent kisses made it all but impossible to think. She did not mind. This was not a time for thinking.

The palms of her hands told her the width of his shoulders, the coiled strength in his arms, the softness of his black hair where it curled over the edge of his starched cravat.

He was like her, she realized. He had not cut his hair to a more fashionable length, nor had he shaved his jaw to appear more respectable. He was none of those things.

He was wild and untamed and devastatingly handsome. The starch in his cravat was not for Society, but for *her*.

The pristine tailcoat, the polished boots, the iridescent waistcoat of jade and emerald, dreams and battles. He had chosen this outfit with the same care that she had chosen her own. Not to impress the world, but the one person who mattered within it.

She gasped as his tongue licked into her mouth, tasting her, knowing her ever more intimately. When she did the same, he growled and pulled her even closer. Her bosom touched his chest. It felt overfull and delightfully sensitive.

Being up on her toes to kiss him imbalanced her, giving her no choice but to lean fully into his embrace.

Not that she'd ever had a choice. As soon as she'd received his note, she knew she would kiss him. If he hadn't pulled her into his embrace, she would have had no choice but to do so herself.

She couldn't stand the separation any longer. Not just the wretched hours they spent away from one another, but any time so much as an arm's width separated them.

She wanted every moment of every day to be just like this. Bodies pressed too tightly together to tell where one ended and the other began. Lips melded, tongues clashing. His hands plunged in her hair and hers in his.

This was living. This was *life*. All the rest was practice, an insipid copy of what they'd found here together.

They were stronger as one. More complete. More combustible. Her entire body tingled as if any moment the heat they were generating might truly erupt into flames.

She longed to rip off her spencer, her gown, her shift. It was too hot in here for clothing. How might his shoulders feel without this tailcoat? His chest, without the waistcoat? What if their bodies had nothing between them but air, and then not even that?

With trembling fingers, she reached for his cravat. A small knot or two, a few pesky buttons, and she might learn more than she'd dreamed of Max and his kisses. The fire between them would—

"Oh!" came a startled female voice.

Bryony leapt away from Max. Her heart skipped madly in her chest. She turned to face a woman about her own age standing just inside Max's open doorway with a key in her hand.

Approximate age was the only thing Bryony seemed to have in common with the new arrival. This woman was beautiful. Femininity incarnate. High cheekbones, darkly-lashed eyes, thick ebony hair that curled into lustrous ringlets of its own accord. She did not look as though she had stepped in from the rain, but rather out of the pages of a magazine. Not a real woman, but an artist's ideal come to life.

"Frances," Max growled in warning. "I instructed you not to visit today."

"Why do you think I came?" the gorgeous woman replied without the slightest repentance and thrust her hand toward Bryony. "You must be the evil siren. I'm Frances, Max's sister."

Amid the avalanche of competing thoughts tumbling through her mind, Bryony managed to grasp the dainty fingers before her and give a firm shake as she'd seen her father do on occasion after a successful business dealing.

Had she somehow engaged in a silent transaction with Max's sister? She might have thought to curtsey rather than shake hands, had a regrettable spurt of envy not convinced her the unexpected visitor was a different type of woman entirely.

She felt her cheeks redden. "I thought you were—"

"—his twin," Frances finished with a laugh. "We hear that all the time. I should be offended, since he is two years my elder. I am only six-and-twenty."

Bryony glanced from Max to Frances and back again. Mortification heated her neck.

Of course. The same dark hair, the same dark eyelashes, the same high cheekbones. The same utter disregard for anyone else's rules or expectations.

"Pleased to meet you," she stammered, catching a glimpse of her upside-down bonnet from the corner of her eye.

It was probably too late to bother picking it up from its position on the floor across the room in a weak attempt toward propriety. There would be no explaining away what Frances had seen as anything other than what it was. With luck, she had only seen the kiss, and not Bryony's passion-drunk desire to turn it into something more.

"Max hasn't said a word," Frances whispered. "He must still be suffering your Medusa effect."

Bryony blinked in confusion, then felt her cheeks heat anew in sudden understanding. He did not see her as a hideous monster, but as a woman who could turn him hard as stone with a mere glance.

Delighted, she shot him a saucy look over her shoulder. "Smart men like powerful women."

"Frances was just leaving," Max said, scowling at his sister. "Goodbye, Frances. Thank you for the short visit. Leave your key on the table and don't come back."

Frances ignored him and threw herself onto his sofa to grin up at them. "Don't mind me. This has been most illuminating. I always wondered what your business meetings were like. No wonder you two spend so much time at the office."

Max stiffened in offense. "I have never before—"

"He's *timid*?" Frances gasped in mock horror.

"Gentlemanly," Bryony corrected primly.

Frances snorted at the idea. "Of course."

"Off the couch," Max said, voice tight. He

pointed from his sister to the exit. "Out the door."

Frances paid this no attention. Her focus was on Bryony. "He says you're an evil genius. Something about turning a greater profit in a fortnight than any of the zanies he invests with could hope to turn in a year."

Bryony beamed with pride in Max's direction.

He glowered at them both.

"One does what one can," she demurred. Frances was a delight. "I'm afraid I don't know much about you. Max has refused my requests for us to meet."

"He has refused mine as well," Frances said, casting her brother a chastening glance. She turned back to Bryony. "Not much to say about me, I'm afraid. Humdrum by comparison. I'm a seamstress and haven't time for anything else."

"She's the most brilliant woman I know," Max contradicted quickly.

His sister widened her eyes in false innocence. "Hm. Cleverer than Bryony?"

His face twisted in consternation when he realized there was no satisfactory reply that could cover both women.

Bryony patted his arm. "It's not your fault. Sisters always win."

"That's what I tell him," Frances whispered.

"For the record," Max said at last. "My sister is more than a seamstress. She's a prodigy."

"I adore prodigies," Bryony exclaimed with sincere admiration. "What is your specialty?"

"Reading," Frances said dryly. "Max should try it sometime."

"She has near-perfect recall," he continued as if his sister hadn't spoken. "Queen of esoteric facts. She has encyclopedic knowledge of the flora and fauna of most European countries. Fran can recite the members of every major world dynasty for as far back as there is written record."

"I'm primarily the queen of Gothic novels," Bryony admitted, impressed. "When I'm not playing with numbers. It doesn't seem nearly as useful. What do you do with all your knowledge?"

"Nothing," Frances said with a little shrug.

"She gets it from our mother." Max cast her a fond expression. "Mother not only taught Fran to sew, but also the joy of reading. When one of them would suffer cramps in their fingers too painful to go on, one would read aloud while the other sewed. It became a habit. They took turns with each book to keep it interesting, improving their minds during every break."

"It doesn't sound like a break," Bryony admitted. "It sounds like a lot of hard work, interspersed with moments of slightly more enjoyable work. Do you enjoy sewing?"

"I'm competent at it," Frances replied noncommittally.

"She's an artist," Max corrected. "She crafted the waistcoat I'm wearing right now."

"I sew all your clothes, if we're adhering to technicalities," Frances said with a grin. "Max is my best-paying client."

"And your most handsome one, I've no doubt." Bryony raked her gaze down Max's perfectly tailored form in appreciation. "He's right. You are an artist."

"I would rather be doing almost anything else," Frances admitted. "It *is* work. But I've sewn twenty of my six-and-twenty years, and if I am fortunate, will do so for forty more."

Max folded his arms over his chest. "Unnecessary. I've told you a hundred times—"

"Go make tea," Frances ordered. "You're being a rude host."

"I didn't invite you," he pointed out.

"But I'm here and I'm thirsty." She waved him out of the room. "Tea. Please. I promise to be nice to Medusa. *Someone* ought to be. Have you read the tale?"

The glare he sent her was highly skeptical. After a silent standoff, Max sighed and made his way to the kitchen.

Bryony took the armchair opposite Frances. "I am intrigued to discover we share an unusual characteristic. I too have a talent I would rather not use. I thought I was the only one. I feel so... ungrateful."

"I'm very grateful." Frances slid down the sofa to

arrange herself directly across Bryony. "If it weren't for my sewing, I would not be able to support myself. That's why Max is so angry. He wants me to avail my-self of his riches and never work a day again."

"Why don't you?" Bryony asked.

"Because it's *his* savings. He earned it, not me." Frances's expression was determined. "I am just as capable. I don't wish to be kept by any man, not even my brother. I shall earn my own way if it kills me."

"Are you doing well?" Bryony asked in a softer voice. "Is Max right to worry?"

Frances made a face. "I am doing better than the others who work for the same modiste. She is one of the most popular, and there is no shortage of clients. Most of the profit, however, never leaves her ac-counts."

Bryony frowned. "Is there anything to be done about it?"

"Max wants me to open my own shop." Frances wrinkled her nose.

Bryony nodded. "But that would require an even greater commitment to a career you do not enjoy."

"And a loan to get started," Frances said with a grimace. "That's part of the problem."

Bryony's eyes widened in surprise. "Max won't loan you money?"

"Correct. He will only give it to me." Frances's eyes were fierce. "He won't let me earn my own way."

Bryony thought this over.

"If I had the money, I would loan it to you with interest," she promised.

Frances grinned. "And I would accept every cent, if I wished to deal with clients, manage a shop, settle accounts, and still sew all day."

Fair enough.

"What would you rather do?" Bryony asked.

Frances gave a crooked smile. "Be paid to read all day?"

"We can wish," Bryony agreed with feeling.

"I have had one impossible wish come true," Frances admitted. "I presume I have you to thank that Max owns colors again."

Bryony blinked. "He didn't own any colors?"

"He never came out of mourning after our mother died, because he felt he had failed a deathbed promise to keep me safe. It was *not* his fault." Frances blinked rapidly. "An armband wasn't enough. He swore never to wear colors again until he had a reason to, and that reason would be that he and I had made it. No longer dependent on or beholden to anyone else."

Bryony bit her lip. She was part of the reason that hadn't happened. No wonder he was so desperate to procure the deed.

"Whatever you're thinking," Frances said firmly, "you're wrong. Max kept his word until this past month, when he met you. The only possible explanation for him to wear colors again after all this time, is that you've given him a reason to finally see beauty in the world again."

Bryony's throat grew thick. She did not deserve compliments.

Max strode into the room with a tea tray and a scowl. "You're whispering. It's troubling behavior. I presume I'm superfluous now."

"I am the one who is superfluous, and ought to be going." Bryony rose on unsteady feet. "I do love your sister, Max. You are more fortunate than you realize."

"I can hear you," Frances stage-whispered. "I'm still right here."

"I am treating you as my family treats me," Bryony told her. "There is no greater pleasure than to be spoken about like an object when one is present in the same room."

"I preemptively dislike your family," Frances said sorrowfully.

"Just my parents," Bryony said quickly. "The rest of my family is quite charming."

A wonderful idea sang through Bryony's veins.

As much as her mother frustrated her, she had also gifted Bryony with the key piece of clout that had afforded all the Grenville siblings not just a secure place in Society, but also an achievement they could be proud of. Something that brought joy. Something they could share with others.

"You should come to the family musicale," she

said in a rush, excitement causing her to trip over her words. "Both of you. I can secure your invitations. The festivities will be held in my parents' home to-morrow night. The salon is often standing room only, so I advise you to come a little early. You'll also have a chance to meet my—"

"No," Max said curtly, his tone bricking neither argument nor explanation. "We will not be anywhere your family might be found."

The unexpected rejection of her heartfelt offer stole Bryony's breath. Her eyes pricked with heat.

"Why?" she asked quietly. "You've no interest in meeting them?"

"I've no interest in wasting time. You and I might have a moment here or there in the shadows, but that is all it will ever be. A diversion, nothing more. Cer-tainly nothing that would require meeting families. Whatever you're thinking might happen... you're wrong."

Frances gasped.

"I see," Bryony said, her lips tight. She swept her bonnet up from the floor and marched out the door, into the cold, and out of their lives.

She would not wait around to be hurt a second time.

Chapter 14

*T*he secluded, soundproof office that had once been Max's refuge from the outside world was now his private hell.

Life wasn't peaceful without Bryony. It was lonely. The journals she'd been studying were still stacked on the settee. The place he had started to consider hers, right where she had left it.

Even if those volumes were the only item out of place in the entire office, he wouldn't put them away.

Putting them away would feel like admitting she was never coming back.

His stomach clenched. He hadn't seen her in days. Ninety-eight hours, if one were to be specific. It felt like a lifetime.

If a few days without her were this hard, what would it feel like when the month was through and she was gone for good?

He pushed the thought away. He couldn't think about that. There were figures that needed to be summed. Plans that needed to be made.

Bryony would be back.

He hoped.

Damn it all, there was no question that he had handled the situation with her family musicale badly.

It wasn't that he wished to keep their burgeoning attachment—or whatever it was—a secret. It was that they couldn't have a relationship at all. Not as lovers; not as friends.

He should never have kissed her. He was right to have turned down the invitation. Nevertheless, he felt like a monster. He was frustrated Bryony didn't see that she was asking for something impossible. She had been thinking with her heart, instead of imagining what the reaction would have been if he had actually accepted.

True, he was no longer a dock worker. He was now something better. Something worse.

The same gentlemen who revered him in his club, who lined up to visit his dark throne deep in the bowels of the Cloven Hoof, would not treat him the same when bathed in the glittering candlelight of crystal chandeliers. Not where they were the kings.

Max had fought hard to gain what respect he had, earn what money he had, garner what success he'd had. If transferring the Cloven Hoof and its property into his name would be visible proof that he'd achieved success... Being snubbed and ridiculed by Bryony's peers right in front of her would be even more incontrovertible proof that he had gained nothing after all.

Only a fool would put himself in such a position.

The absolute worst possible person to fall in love with would be someone who made his many differences seem all the starker. Someone whose world would either cast him bodily from it or swallow his soul in darkness.

His heart skipped, and he set down his plume with shaking fingers.

Fall in love? Foolish notion. No matter how much he liked Bryony, he was in no danger of love. He knew their time was limited. Days, numbered.

No matter how much he might wish otherwise.

His throat tightened. The reason he felt so conflicted over turning down her invitation, the reason his gut cramped with each memory of the flash of hurt that had crumpled her hopeful face until she could disguise the pain, was because he held her happiness on par with his own.

A faint knock sounded from outside the Cloven Hoof. Max frowned. The club had closed an hour ago.

Was it Bryony? Had she lost her key?

He leaped from his chair and dashed into the corridor just as the knock sounded a second time. He paused.

The sound had not come from the rear exit leading to the alleyway, but from the primary entrance at the front.

Frowning, he strode through the club to the main door and threw it open wide.

A lad in ill-fitting clothing and a too-big top hat stared back at him.

Not a lad.

His sister.

"What the devil?" Max spluttered.

"So this is the Cloven Hoof," Frances said as she brushed past him into the primary salon. "I can't see a thing. Consider lighting a few candles for your guest."

"Why are you here?" he demanded. "*How* are you here?"

"I received an invitation. And this outfit." She gestured at her preposterous ensemble. "This is where the driver brought me."

Max buried his face in his hands. "Good Lord."

This had to be Bryony's doing. But for what purpose? What could she mean by it?

"I found a candle," Frances called. "Shall I use this to light the others?"

Max reached behind the bar for a tinderbox and then lit the spare taper closest to the door. Without a word, he set about lighting all the other candles until the interior of the Cloven Hoof was as bright as it ever managed to get.

"No wonder you only wear black," Frances said, impressed. "Can the players even read their cards?"

"It's not that dark," he groused. "What exactly was in your invitation? When did you receive it? Did she say anything else?"

"She?" Frances asked. "It was signed 'Basil Q. Jones.'"

"And you *came*?" Max thundered.

"It did say 'Bryony' beneath that, in parentheses," Frances mused, then turned toward the gaming tables. "I'm inside a den of iniquity! I never thought this day would come. Start the tour, dear brother."

Max clamped his teeth together. He wanted to be angry. He *ought* to be angry. But Bryony had managed a feat that he had not.

Since the Cloven Hoof's inception, Frances had wanted to visit. He hadn't allowed her to do so, because he felt such a risk too dangerous.

The last time the topic had come up, he *had* offered to bring Fran after hours, and she had turned him down. He didn't blame her. Too little, too late.

Basil Q. Jones to the rescue.

Max gave up trying to fight Fate.

"This is the bar," he said, gesturing behind him. "It previously contained a disproportionate quantity of Bordeaux and Champagne, but once Bryony reframed our stock of French wine as 'spoils of war,' it became the only thing anyone will drink, no matter the price."

Frances's eyes widened. "Bryony did that?"

He smirked. "I believe her exact words were something like, 'We beat Boney and we'll drink his land dry. Every bubbly drop of it.'"

Frances grinned in satisfaction. "I do like her."

So did Max.

He crossed to the gaming tables and explained each one in turn. Its number, according to the new index he and Bryony had devised. Its game and number of players. Whether there was a schedule change on certain days. Which ones were more profitable than others, and what steps Bryony had invented to exploit existing opportunities for higher gains.

Frances nodded, rapt.

Max was waxing poetic on the last of the tables when he realized he had spent the past quarter hour deep in a monologue about all the ways Bryony had not only made his life easier, but personally changed his club for the better.

"So... she makes herself useful?" Frances asked with a knowing smile. "It sounds like this club belongs to both of you."

Max's smile died.

His sister's insightful comment had hit a bit too close to home.

The Cloven Hoof did not belong to both him and Bryony. The property currently belonged to Bryony alone. If she wished, she could shut it down at any time.

He didn't think she *would*, mostly because such a counter-intuitive action would be an irresponsible financial decision not supported by available facts. When it came to business, Bryony could be trusted to take the most logical path.

However, it did not require an analytical genius to realize selling Max such a lucrative property made absolutely no business sense at all. Bryony would be foolish to give up her best advantage.

And Bryony was far from foolish.

Frances crossed from the gaming salon to the seating area. "What is the purpose of this room? Are these tables numbered, too?"

Before Max could answer, the rear exit opened and Bryony struggled inside with a slender wooden crate.

Her hair was tucked inside a top hat not unlike the one his sister wore. Her greatcoat fit just as badly, her nankeen trousers a little too long, her smile just as wide.

She looked more beautiful every time he saw her.

He crossed his arms and scowled at her. "I knew you were behind this."

"Of course I was behind this," she said cheerfully as she placed an oblong case wrapped in linen down on the floor.

He would make his inquiries into this new mystery in a moment.

"How the devil did you determine my sister's address?" he demanded.

Bryony hooked her top hat on the wall and raised her brows. "Have you met my brother?"

"Thank you so much for sending for me." Frances bounded over to Bryony with the excitement of a newborn kitten. "I love everything I've seen so far, but Max gives a dreadful tour. Won't you show me about?"

"I'll do my best." Self-consciously, Bryony gave a crooked smile. "It's not my club. Everything you see here, Max built. He is the brains behind every detail."

Frances shot a knowing look over her shoulder at Max. "Is that so? Have you not been helping with the wine and the tables?"

Bryony shrugged out of her greatcoat and draped it over her arm. Max watched her lead Fran back down the corridor toward the entrance, not realizing she had just come from there.

"I might tune where I can, but the foundation was already here." Bryony frowned and corrected herself. "More than a foundation. The Cloven Hoof was blossoming before I ever stepped through the door. Do you see this bar?"

Frances nodded innocently. "Seems the sort of venue that would only sell French wine."

Bryony waved this away. "We did have a few extra cases by mistake, but that was solved in a trice. As is everything. Max quite brilliantly keeps a few bottles on hand from every part of the world. Whether your taste runs to ales brewed here in London, wine or whiskey smuggled from the darkest corners of Europe, he can meet your every desire. This is not just a gambling den, but a place where wishes come true."

Max's chest warmed.

"And these tables?" Frances asked. "Were you involved in determining their function?"

"I shared ideas," Bryony admitted grudgingly. "But your brother had already nearly maximized every bit of potential."

Frances arched her brows. "How so?"

"He purchased the perfect tables for every kind of game, and is meticulous about their upkeep and condition," Bryony explained. "In other gambling dens, warped surfaces and rickety chairs lead to an unpleasant gaming experience. Not here in the Cloven Hoof. Your brother has ensured his players enjoy every comfort. They have no reason to leave, which increases their satisfaction as well as the club's profits."

Max tried not to grin.

"And this room?" Frances asked as they crossed to the more secluded conversation nook.

Bryony's eyes brightened. "That is yet another stroke of your brother's genius. He—"

Max did not follow. He no longer could.

Her unscripted responses to his sister's queries

had rooted him in place.

Bryony didn't see his gaming hell solely as some investment opportunity. She saw it as the achievement it was. Recognized details he hadn't even shared with her.

Of course she would know what other gambling clubs were like. She must have seen a dozen similar proposals before choosing to finance his. She had held him to a higher standard before their contract had even been signed. He ran a hand through his hair.

She thought he was brilliant. Successful. She was proud of the Cloven Hoof. Proud of *him*. His throat tightened.

When they were alone in his office, she had always made him feel like he could be himself. No disclaimers or apologies required. That was part of her magic. This was something else. Something more.

This was how she always thought of him. He didn't need to prove himself to her. She already thought him worthy.

Max was the one who kept pushing Bryony away. He gazed at her from across the room. His fixation on all the ways in which he and his sister were outsiders had caused him to make Bryony an outsider as well.

He had kept her on the fringes of his small circle for long enough.

It was past time to let her in.

As he watched her chatter animatedly with his sister, the stone surrounding his heart gave a little crack. No matter what happened with Bryony, no matter what happened with the property, he feared he was a changed man. He clamped his teeth together.

Of course, he would still stop at nothing to get his hands on the deed.

He would not be able to rest until the Cloven Hoof was fully his. Only then could he begin to meet Bryony as an equal. As a man who had made his own way and had something to show for it. Who didn't need anyone else because he already had it all.

Once he achieved that goal, he would finally respect himself, and deserve the respect of others. He could relax. And perhaps spend more time with Bryony.

"What's in the case?" he asked suspiciously.

Bryony stopped talking to Frances and turned to grin at him. "Your musicale."

He blinked. "My what?"

She motioned for them to join her in the office, where she laid the case on his desk and opened it to reveal a stringed instrument of exquisite craftsmanship.

"Your violin," he said in awe.

Frances's mouth fell open.

Bryony placed the delicate instrument to her

chin and motioned for him and his sister to take their seats on the settee.

No sooner had they done so, then Bryony touched her bow to the strings.

Max barely registered his sister's audible gasp at the beauty that burst into the air.

He was lost inside Bryony's soaring melody. Her music filled the room. Vibrated up the walls and through the furniture. Sent shivers down the back of his spine.

Her violin was not a separate entity, but an extension of her soul. Both delicate and strong. Gentle and loud. Powerful enough to bring tears to one's eyes. He could not look away.

No wonder the Grenville musicales were the most celebrated event of the *ton*. Max had heard when Bryony's eldest sister joined an opera house. Rumor had it that her voice was unlike any other. Her fame as a soprano had already reached far beyond London's borders.

He hadn't realized Bryony was every bit as gifted. That she hadn't been inviting Frances and him to some dull aristocratic get-together, but to witness her tearing open her chest and letting her heart fly out through the strings.

Never before had he heard such music. Nor would he. Bryony was unparalleled, her style as unique as she was. That was what elevated her above all the rest.

When the melody finally faded away, it took the air from his lungs with it.

Silence filled the room.

"Was it all right?" Bryony asked after a long moment.

Frances threw herself at Bryony's knees. "Marry me!"

Bryony's shoulders shook with laughter as she pulled Frances to her feet. "I shall consider your request, my lady. In the meantime, I hope you are not offended if I ask you to settle for being my honorary sister instead."

"Accepted," Frances said instantly and hopped onto the desk at Bryony's side. "May I see it? How does it work?"

Bryony immediately allowed her to touch the violin's intricate wooden curves.

Max finally found his breath. *This* was why she had invited his sister here tonight. To prove that the Cloven Hoof wouldn't crumble if another woman stepped inside its doors, yes. But more than that, her extraordinary gift with music was something she wanted to share with both of them. Not just with Max.

To Bryony, Frances was part of the package, too.

Max's heart beat so fast he feared the women might hear it from across the room.

Two women in lad's clothing, cooing over an expensive violin in the back of an infamous gaming hell.

When had his life turned so upside-down?

Bryony's eyes met his. It was impossible to keep a smile from curving his lips.

She was the reason. The tinderbox who had burst into his darkness and lit the first spark.

With her, there was more than light. There was music.

She gave him a crooked grin. "Are you wishing you came to the musicale?"

"Yes," he answered honestly. "Wishing it were possible. I would have loved to share it with you, now that I know what I'm missing."

"There will be other soirées," she said, her voice hesitant.

After a moment, he shook his head. "You know as well as I do that I don't belong there. All my presence could do is cause you scandal."

"I know."

To his surprise, the flash of sorrow in her eyes indicated she truly had realized what she was asking. That accepting such an invitation would be a one-time possibility. Never to be repeated.

Her smile wobbled. "But having you there would have been worth it."

Max was not so sure. If he used up his one chance, there would be no more sneaking away to be together. No more Bryony. He was not ready to give her up just yet.

"Now that your musicale is over, I suppose your nights have returned to a busy schedule of husband-hunting?" he heard himself ask.

Frances's head jerked up with interest.

"Something like that," Bryony admitted, as she slid from the desk. "Mother has me in ringlets and pastels nearly every day of the week."

Each word sliced through his heart. Soon enough, some other man would have the sort of life with her that part of Max wished he were in a position to offer. He might not be a suitor, but he could give her something else. A reminder of *their* connection. The reason she was here.

He took a step in her direction. "A dreadful week indeed. Are you certain there's been nothing diverting at all to break up the monotony?"

"Lambley did remind me I have a standing invitation to attend his masquerades. I've never been." She took another step closer until the toes of her boots brushed his. She licked her lips. "I would rather be here at the Cloven Hoof with you."

A wild ray of hope wriggled into his brain.

Lambley's masquerades.

Open invitation.

Max, too, had never been. Never previously had a reason to attend. That reason might be standing right in front of them right now. His heart sped faster at the thought.

He took her hands. "What if neither of us were

here? What if we were masked revelers on a candlelit dance floor instead?"

Bryony gazed back at him, speechless.

Frances backed away toward the door. "And... what if I found a hackney to remove me as far as possible from this intimate moment?"

Bryony laughed and let go of Max's hands. "I have to get my Stradivarius home, anyway. Not only is it the most expensive item I own, I half expect it's the only reason my mother still keeps me around."

She slipped on her greatcoat and top hat, then wrapped up her case and moved toward the door.

He stared after her in disbelief. Was she going to leave him once more without so much as goodbye?

She *was.*

Max dashed outside to stop her, not bothering with a coat or hat. Wet weather didn't matter. Only *she* did.

He caught her between the silver moon and the falling raindrops. This might be his last chance to change her mind. He pressed his lips to hers in a kiss so desperate and so deep he hoped she would remember the taste forevermore, whenever she thought of this night.

"The masquerade is a week from tonight," he said between kisses. "Please think about joining me."

She rescued her fallen top hat and rose to give him another kiss. "The only thing I ever think about is... joining you."

When she sauntered off, it was Max who was left
to remember her parting words again and again for
the rest of the night.

Chapter 15

*F*or the first time in her life, Bryony was having difficulty focusing on numbers.

Possibly because she was sharing the desk with Max, and no matter how hard she squinted at the neat columns of numbers in the journal, all of her senses were tuned to him.

The way his dark hair fell over his forehead as he bent over some piece of documentation in concentration. The way his lips tightened in concentration. The quiet strength in his hands, whose familiar fingers had once been in her hair, and stroking her cheek.

"You are a terrible influence on my sister," he said presently.

She grinned. "Frances needed a fault."

Bryony was not at all surprised to discover his sister just as competent, confident, and marvelous as

Max. Their parents must have been extraordinary individuals. She wished she could have known them. The seamstress mother, who instilled her daughter with a love of books and learning. The father who...

She swung her head toward Max. She had no idea who or how his father had been. Max had never said.

"Your mother was a seamstress," she began, leaning toward him in interest.

"Mm," he responded without glancing up from his document.

She pressed on, undaunted. "And your father?"

"Not a seamstress."

No further explanation.

She should not have asked. The air between them had filled with awkwardness.

"Had he a phobia of needles?" she tried to jest.

At this, Max did look up. "Father had no time for phobias. He worked on the docks from the time he was born until the day he died. The only times I saw him were when he came home with each month's salary, and when he was finally too weak to rise from his sickbed."

Bryony's chest pounded in sympathy. She hadn't meant to dredge up painful memories. This one sounded awful. She might know what it was like never to see one's father, but hers was still alive and hid himself away in a comfortable armchair in a comfortable office in his comfortable townhouse, well protected from the elements.

It was not the same at all.

Max had rarely seen his father out of necessity, not choice. That made it simultaneously more palatable and a thousand times worse. His father was the sort of man willing to work himself to death if it meant bringing home enough coin to live on for his wife and children. A man who valued his family more than himself.

And now he was gone.

She swallowed. "I..."

"I'm not ashamed of him," Max's proud gaze did not waver. "As soon as I was able, I did the same. I would do it again. I would be working the docks right now, if Basil Q. Jones hadn't taken a risk on a dream no one else considered worth the investment."

Her throat grew tight. How silly her struggles seemed in comparison.

She had lamented the diminutive seed money she had used to launch six fruitful years of pseudonymous investment, but she had been afforded a privileged starting point. Excess baubles to sell. Pin money she hadn't bothered to spend.

All this time, she had considered her financial success something she had done with her hands, with her brain, solely on her own recognizance.

But it wasn't true.

Her lowest rung had been a step on the ladder far above any that someone like Max could hope to reach.

And yet he had tried anyway.

"It wasn't a risk," she said softly. "Basil Q. Jones analyzed all pertinent details and determined that of all the schemes vying for his interest, one held more merit than the rest. Basil didn't see 'potential' in you and your proposal. He recognized the certainty of success."

The corner of Max's mouth twitched, but his half-smile failed to reach his eyes. "Our friend Basil had more confidence than I did. All I had was desperation and a wild, foolish dream."

"'Foolish' only describes those who didn't believe in you." She gestured about them. "We are sitting in your foolish dream right now. We met when I snuck *inside* of it. Your dream now has hundreds of happy clients. Thousands. Your dream has employees. Your dream has allowed *others* to dream. Your dream has changed reality."

Max stared back at her without speaking. As if he did not dare to.

"Investing in you wasn't a stroke of good fortune," she said softly. "You deserved it. You deserve every good thing that has ever happened, and a thousand more. You and your dreams are as worthy as anyone else's."

His lips twisted. "Tell that to the gods ruling over all the other gentlemen's clubs. The benevolent lords who blackballed me unanimously."

"Which gentlemen's clubs?" she demanded. Righteous anger on his behalf shot through her veins.

Amusement flickered across Max's face. "All of them."

"I'll have Heath fix it," she said immediately. "My brother—"

"Under no circumstances." Max's expression was hard and final. "If they don't want me, I don't want them. And be honest. You're not surprised they don't want me."

Bryony grit her teeth together.

His smirk was answer enough.

Blast it all. There must be a way. She wanted to ask when he had applied. After his fame and fortune as ruler of the Cloven Hoof, or before it became the most sought-after gaming hell in London?

But he was right. It wouldn't have mattered.

He had no title, no aristocratic blood. He had climbed as high as someone from his background could go. And it still fell short. Nothing he might do or achieve would make him good enough to move in her circles.

"They are opinionated, insular idiots," she said at last. "It doesn't matter what they think."

"I know," Max said, his gaze even. "I didn't expect them to allow me in."

She frowned. "Then why..."

"I wanted to force them to have my name on

their lips," he said fiercely. "To speak out loud from the sanctity of their club why I wasn't worthy to join them. And then drive their fancy coaches with ancient family crests over here to my door in order to beg entrance into my world."

She straightened. "You blackballed them?"

"Best day of my life," he said with satisfaction.

Bryony grinned back. "Good."

Her smile faltered when she realized it meant her own father was likely one of the men who had voted against him. One of the many privileged gentlemen who believed he could then walk into the Cloven Hoof as if he owned the place, only to be turned away at the door.

Perhaps that was the real reason why Max has been disgusted to learn she was a Grenville.

She couldn't blame him.

His story gripped her heart. He had been born into poverty. Raised by his mother. Worked on the docks. Made more of himself than anyone of his acquaintance ever thought him capable of achieving.

Not only wasn't he searching for some rich, high-class savior to bestow greatness by association and thereby elevate his worth.... He didn't need a savior of any kind.

Or her.

Her chest thumped in sudden understanding.

She wasn't sitting across from him at this desk because she had broken in, because she had been his first investor, because she owned the deed.

She was here because he hadn't blackballed her.

It was *she* who'd had to prove herself to him. To be worthy of his time. Of his trust. All her contributions were incidental. The journals spread out before her proved how competent and clever he was completely on his own.

She looked around the meticulously ordered interior. This was his dream, not hers. If she cared about him at all, she ought not stand in his way.

He *deserved* the deed.

She had no right to keep it from him.

That he didn't already possess it was a technicality. Her presumptiveness, her self-interest, was all that kept her from giving in. She was so afraid that once he possessed the deed, he wouldn't need her anymore. No, not fear. It was the truth. She was delaying the inevitable.

Her throat tightened.

Giving Max his land was the right thing to do. She might wish to be part of the Cloven Hoof, but he *needed* the Cloven Hoof.

And as for Bryony?

Perhaps there was something else out there for someone like her.

"What are you thinking about?" he asked.

She dropped her gaze to the journals. "Nothing. Arithmetic."

"You haven't scribbled a single number in the

past quarter hour." He leaned back in his chair and crossed his arms.

Bryony went with a half-truth. "I was thinking about Almack's."

He flinched and immediately shuttered his expression. "You're thinking about ensnaring a titled gentleman?"

"I'm thinking about burning Almack's to the ground and remaking it in the Cloven Hoof's image." She squinted into the distance as she imagined how wonderful it would be. "Instead of rigid rules for entry, I would let everyone in. Perhaps then love matches wouldn't be so rare."

"And... that is why no one will ever allow you to become a Patroness." His posture relaxed.

She shrugged. "I know."

"It is an interesting idea," he admitted. "An assembly room wherein everyone is allowed to assemble. But I doubt it would have the effect you intend. Those who prefer exclusivity and showing the world how much better they are than others would not attend."

Bryony wrinkled her nose. "Would you want them to?"

"I think you're very unusual," he said softly. "You are able to see much more of the world than just the sliver visible to most people."

She stared back at him. What she cared about most was the fearless, bullheaded man right before her eyes.

"I brought something," she blurted.

His gaze turned suspicious. "What is it?"

Something she'd been carrying about for a week, undecided on whether to give it to him. Something meant to be square, and meant to be beautiful, and meant to prove exactly how much he was starting to mean.

Instead, her grand gesture was ugly, lumpy, and indeterminate in function. Perhaps a little too on-the-nose for a gift that reflected the heart.

Pulse racing, she pulled the misshapen cushion from a bag at her feet and placed it on his desk.

He stared at it for a long moment without blinking. "It's..."

She took pity on him. "A pillow."

He nodded sagely. "For me?"

She nodded. "There's more to the story. You may find it difficult to believe that this is the first sewing project I've ever completed in my life."

"I'm flattered to be the recipient of such a unique honor," he murmured. "Was it meant to be a pillow all along?"

"It was meant to be a sampler," she admitted. "But the pattern was bigger than anticipated and the seamstress significantly less competent than one might desire, which culminated in the resulting work being a bit too... *asymmetrical* to fit in any frame. So I added a backside and stuffed it with feathers."

"I like backsides," he said. "Especially yours."

She flushed with pleasure. He was looking at her like he wanted to kiss her again. There was nothing she wanted more. Well, almost nothing. First, she wanted him to accept his gift. It meant more to her than he knew. She bit her lip.

He had yet to so much as touch the pillow. Either because he feared it far too delicate to be manhandled or because he was afraid it carried leprosy.

She hoped her nervousness did not show in her eyes.

"Are those horns?" he asked politely. "The red bits in the middle?"

She pulled a sheet of foolscap from her bag and set it beside the pillow.

"I took the liberty of preparing a legend to aid in interpretation." She pointed at the center of her needlework. "This part says 'Cloven Hoof.' These over here are horns, as you correctly noted. Over there is a forked tail. This is a glass of ale. Those are playing cards."

"And the..." He wiggled his fingers at the tangles of thread demarking the perimeter.

She nodded. "The gray curlicues at the top are smoke and the orange ones at the bottom are hellfire."

"It's beautiful," he pronounced. "Much too beautiful to use. It is a work of art that should be displayed prominently, so that all might enjoy it as much as I do."

"If only Mother were here," Bryony murmured. "I *told* her it was art."

He gingerly picked up the pillow and carried it to his bookshelf, where he made a place for it between Walpole and Wollstonecraft on the topmost shelf. A focal position, where anyone entering the office would have no choice but to bask in its glory.

Bryony grinned to herself. The dear man would be explaining his choice in artwork for the rest of his days.

"Perhaps I have a future as a seamstress," she mused aloud.

To his credit, Max did not choke with laughter. "Perhaps you can apprentice Frances."

"She is too smart for that," Bryony admitted.

She returned her gaze to the numbers before her, but her runaway thoughts were now on Max's sister.

That Frances did not wish for her brother or any man to run her life was something Bryony very much understood. Yet a woman in Frances's position had few options. It would be difficult to divine an acceptable way out.

Fortunately, Bryony had a gift for difficult calculations.

Chapter 16

*T*hree days later, Max still caught himself gazing across his perfectly organized office at the hideous pillow up on his shelf. It looked like she'd fed a cat spools of colored thread and affixed the resulting hairballs to fine linen.

Never had he seen anything more misshapen in his life.

But Bryony had made it for him, so it held not only a dedicated place in his office, but also in his heart.

Even if he could never tell her so himself.

He slid his gaze to the far side of his desk. She had sent him a letter just that morning. A letter he had been studiously ignoring, and simultaneously obsessing over.

She had met his sister and wanted him to meet

hers. The note was an invitation to the St. Giles School for Girls. Some sort of activity they were planning for two o'clock this afternoon.

It was currently a quarter past two.

He could blame his absence on being too busy at the club. It wouldn't open for a few more hours, but there was always more to be done than time in which to do it. She would not be surprised by such an excuse at all.

Nor would she believe him.

Max glared at the invitation. He had been adamant about not getting too close. Not crossing the line. Ever since that afternoon in front of Gunter's Tea Shop, he had sworn off public encounters altogether. With Bryony, anyway.

But this was not public. It was a private boarding school. In the middle of a rookery. A world away from the fashionable and the wealthy.

As much as he was trying to keep from entangling himself further by dreaming of a life they could never share... He would love to meet Bryony's sisters.

Max had known her elder brother Heath for many years. Despite being heir to a barony, he had never once put on airs or attempted to put Max in his place.

The other sisters sounded even more unusual, particularly for their class. Now that he knew Bryony's full name, he'd done some investigating of his own. Her oldest sister had caused an enormous scandal by choosing to become an opera singer. And the middle one had apparently opened a high-quality school in the lowest-class part of town.

A rookery was about as neutral a location as Max was likely to get.

Thus decided, he pushed away the pile of accounts he'd been failing to tally and headed outside to flag a hack. In no time at all, the carriage wheels were clomping past Seven Dials and coming up on the old abbey that now held the St. Giles School for Girls.

After paying the driver, Max alighted from the carriage and cautiously approached the front door.

His knock was answered not by Bryony or a butler, but by a twelve-year-old moppet with ginger plaits, a wrinkled pinafore, and a scowl to rival Vigo's when he guarded the Cloven Hoof.

Max cleared his throat, unsure of the next move.

She gazed up at him sullenly.

He met her stare with his own.

At last, she gave an exaggerated sigh. "Calling card?"

Max clenched his empty fingers.

Calling cards were not an affectation he possessed. He had no reason to call upon anyone who might request one of him. Had, in fact, not anticipated being challenged thusly on the broken cobblestones of a rookery.

Even here, he failed to meet expectations.

"Maxwell Gideon," he announced instead, imbuing his voice with his usual confidence and swagger.

"Card room," she muttered bitterly. "Everyone but me. Butler duty is a travesty."

Max blinked and bent his knees to match her height. "Did you say, 'card room?'"

"This way." She made an about-face and strode off down a corridor without waiting to see if he would follow.

Quickly, he stepped across the school's threshold, closed the door behind him, and hurried after the disgruntled redhaired lass stuck on butler duty against her will.

She led him around a staircase and through a wide chamber with a dais that could easily double as a stage and ballroom, then into a secondary salon where at least thirty people sat cross-legged on the floor amidst a hailstorm of fluttering playing-cards.

"Card room," his guide announced and immediately stomped back to her post without properly introducing him.

It was just as well. Max could not tear his gaze from the mêlée within.

Most of the faces he glimpsed belonged to a range of girls as young as six and as old as fourteen. However, this level of chaos had not been caused by children alone. By his count, at least five grown adults were instigating the anarchy.

Heath Grenville, he knew at once. Bryony, of course. The soprano sister, he recognized from the caricatures. The Earl of Wainwright, her husband and a frequent visitor of the Cloven Hoof. And a dark-haired woman who—using his astonishing powers of deduction—must be the sister who had founded the school.

There.

That comprised the entirety of the logical conclusions Max could deduce from the illogical scene before of him.

What the devil they were doing, if indeed there was any method to their madness, was quite beyond his ken. The object of the game appeared to have more to do with keeping cards in the air than in play.

"Max!" Bryony exclaimed in delight and scrambled to her feet.

Given she was in a dress and not trousers, she did so quite elegantly.

He inclined his head in greeting.

She pointed to the dark-haired woman in the center of the room. "May I present my sister, Mrs. Dahlia Spaulding."

When the sister scrambled to *her* feet, Max caught a brief glimpse of trouser bottoms beneath her gown. He could not think of an explanation for such a sartorial choice, and decided in this case it was perhaps best not to seek answers.

Mrs. Spaulding dipped the most flatteringly low

curtsy Max had ever seen in his life.

Come to think of it, he wasn't certain anyone had ever curtsied in his direction before.

He knew that the proper response for a gentleman was to make an elegant leg of his own. As he had never previously been treated as a gentleman, he had not bothered to practice the maneuver.

He regretted that choice now.

Awkwardly, he dipped a little bow toward the headmistress and hoped it did not offend. "My pleasure."

"Children!" Mrs. Spaulding called out. "Pay your respects to Mr. Gideon."

Thirty little girls scrambled to their feet at once and performed picture-perfect curtsies in unison.

Max found himself bowing yet again. His mind fogged at the unexpected turn of events. He had gone from never-been-curtsied-to-before to curtsied-to-by-thirty-women-at-once in the space of a breath.

Bryony headed straight toward him with a sister attached to each elbow. "You've now met Dahlia, the headmistress of this circus. I'd also like you to meet Camellia, whom you may know as Lady Wainwright."

The countess immediately dipped him an even more impressive curtsy than her sister had.

A countess.

Curtsying to *Max*.

He desperately wished he had any idea how to

make a proper leg.

Somehow he managed to bow without disaster.

"Come," Mrs. Spaulding said, motioning him to join the others on the floor. "It's perfect timing. We're just in the middle of a game of cards."

Max hesitated. This truly was an organized game of some kind? And they wanted him to join?

His eyes met the commiserative gazes of the sole two men amongst the roomful of women.

With a knowing look, Lord Wainwright called out, "You'll get used to it."

"I invented this game myself," Heath Grenville added proudly.

"New rule!" shouted a girl who had just tossed an impressive quantity of playing-cards into the air. "It's Mr. Gideon's turn next."

That was a rule?

Before Max could properly discern what was happening, half a dozen students in plaits and pinafores dragged him to the middle of the room, sat him on the carpet, and presented him with a bent pile of playing-cards.

"Er..." he said brilliantly. He ran a gaming hell. He could do this. "How many cards am I meant to deal each person?"

The girls laughed at his apparently ridiculous query. "Molly's rule was to abolish specific counts of any sort, and Beatrice's rule was to get rid of dealing altogether."

"It was?" Max said faintly.

The girls pointed at the pile of playing-cards in his hand. "Louisa's rule is that the number of cards you get is however many you are handed."

"Of course." Defeated, he turned his gaze toward Bryony in supplication.

"Whoever wins a round gets to make a new rule for the game," she told him, eyes sparkling. "That was my rule. Winners are also allowed to toss their playing cards in the faces of their opponents, who may then do the same. The girls have decided that it is your turn. Go ahead when you're ready."

Max gazed back at her in consternation. When he was ready to what, exactly? The alleged explanation had given him absolutely no insight into the actual mechanics of the game.

He turned his cards face up.

All of the girls immediately did the same.

He fanned them in one hand to hide their face value from his dozens of nosy onlookers.

All of the girls did the same.

He narrowed his eyes.

The six-year-old closest to him narrowed hers right back.

Max grinned. Someone's rule must have been, *copy whoever's turn it is.* This could be fun after all. He closed the fan of cards in one sharp movement, creating a crisp rectangular stack, and then placed the entirety atop his head in perfect balance.

With shrieks of merriment, the girls attempted to do the same.

In seconds, the varyingly-sized piles of cards had slid down necks, over ears, into laps, and onto the carpet.

Max was the only one whose pile was still on his head.

"Mr. Gideon wins the round!" shrieked an eight- or nine-year-old toward the back.

"Excellent work, Mr. Gideon," Bryony said with a twinkle in her eyes. "Announce your new rule, and toss your cards at the opponent of your choice."

He retrieved his stack of cards from atop his head and considered his options.

A rule that the winner got to kiss Bryony would backfire very quickly. He would have to save that one for later.

He arched his arm behind his head, clearly prepared to launch his stack of playing-cards into the crowd. "From now on, whoever is the first to be doused in playing cards, must immediately squawk like a chicken."

The girls erupted into peals of laughter.

"Choose me!" shouted one.

"No, me!" screamed another.

With a sudden movement, Max tossed his cards a few inches to his side so that they showered down over Bryony.

"Bok-bok-bok," she crowed, to the girls' delight.

Max found himself laughing as hard as the other students.

In no time at all, he could scarcely believe when the clock turned three and playtime was over.

As the students picked up hundreds of scattered cards and put the room to rights, he realized he could not recall the last time he had laughed so hard or for so long. He very much regretted only arriving in time for the second half of the game.

"Remind me to add this one to the Cloven Hoof," he murmured to Heath deadpan.

"Only if we are there to play, too," his opera singer sister said quickly. "Our brother may have started the game, but the three of us refined it into perfection."

"I'm not sure the Cloven Hoof could handle four Grenvilles at once," Max admitted.

Though he rather wished he could make it happen. Their enthusiasm and good humor were infectious.

"If you're not tired of us yet," Heath said with a smile. "My wife and I are having a dinner party in a week's time, and you are more than welcome to join us."

All of Max's relaxed happiness vanished at the thought. "No."

"Not a *ton* party," Bryony said quickly.

"Small," Heath insisted, his expression sincere. "Friends and family. Which means you qualify."

"If it makes a difference," added the headmistress sister, "our parents cannot make it, so you're spared that gauntlet as well."

Max cleared his throat self-consciously and amended his brusque response. "No, thank you."

He could not. A half hour visit to a rookery was one thing. Descending upon well-heeled ladies and gentlemen bussing cheeks in a Mayfair townhome was quite another. Having Max amongst them would embarrass everyone present.

"Think about it," Bryony murmured, briefly brushing the back of her fingers against his. "Give me your answer tomorrow night, at the masquerade."

He made no promises, for what could he say? He was not the dinner party sort.

Bryony needed a gentleman who deserved her. Not some underworld heathen who would ruin her social status in a heartbeat if an association with him were to be made public.

A stolen evening with her behind the safety of masks would have to be good enough for them both.

Chapter 17

*T*he following night, as Max's hackney inched forward among the impressive queue leading to the Duke of Lambley's sprawling estate, he had plenty of time to second-guess the cursed arrogance that had brought him here tonight.

Given that even his afternoon visit to a rookery wasn't as free from awkward failures in politesse as one might assume, presenting himself at the doorstep of a duke seemed significantly greater hubris.

Despite the elegant black velvet mask his sister had fashioned for him, he felt like a fraud. As if at any moment someone would catch him out and turn him away.

Perhaps the doorman wouldn't believe someone like Max belonged anywhere near the residence of the duke. Perhaps the duke himself had issued his invitation in jest, never expecting Max to take him up on the offer.

He did not *think* these things were true, but they had happened to him before. Countless times, in countless ways.

As a small child he had slowly learned to become suspicious of kind gestures. Every outstretched hand could easily turn into a slap of the face.

But Bryony was inside. Or would be shortly.

He would not disappoint her.

Or at least, he would try not to.

When it was his turn to present himself in the receiving chamber to be inspected by the doorman, Max assumed his customary cloak of hauteur. It was his armor, impenetrable to cruelty and pitying glances. A well-worn shield.

"Gideon!" the doorman exclaimed and clapped him on the shoulder. "I thought Lambley kept your name on the list to tease me. I put five quid on your never leaving the Cloven Hoof."

Relief coursed through Max to recognize the friendly visage of Anthony Fairfax, a one-time regular at his club. He hadn't anticipated any friendly faces but Bryony's.

"Is my name on the list of yeas or the list of nays?" Max joked.

Er, mostly joked.

The doorman chuckled. "The white list, of

course. Lambley runs his parties like you do your gaming hell. His vote is the only one that matters, and you are one of his favorites. He'll be in and out of the cardroom if you'd like to catch him."

"Of course," Max said, as if he had any idea where the cardroom would be in relation to any other. He placed his mask over his face and tied the ribbon tight.

Fairfax moved toward the door. "Ready? I'll announce you."

Max frowned. Announce him? Wasn't the point of a masquerade to be anonym—

Fairfax flung open the door and pushed Max into a glittering world of crystal and chaos, bright colors and swirling costumed bodies.

"Lord X!" Fairfax shouted and closed the door tightly behind Max.

"Lord X!" screamed the crowd, lifting flutes of champagne in cheer.

Max blinked in wonder.

He had not only gained entrance to a duke's residence, passed muster at the gate thanks to a whitelist, but in his first moments inside had already been toasted by two or three hundred of the duke's closest friends. A crowd who hadn't the least idea who Max was. Nor did they seem to care. Tonight, he was apparently known as Lord X. No other information mattered.

A strange sensation tickled down his neck. He

wasn't certain how he felt about being accepted only because he was masked. Part of him wanted to turn around and leave all the hypocrites behind. Another part of him wanted to stay and take every advantage he could.

Particularly if it meant more time with Bryony.

A passing footman expertly placed a glass of champagne in Max's empty hand like a magic fairy distributing candies to children.

That was what this felt like, Max realized. A candy land, a fairy world. Everything was too fast and too bright and too colorful. Nothing was real. No one wished it to be. They were sharing a temporary fantasy from midnight to dawn.

And there was only one woman Max fantasized about.

He stepped away from the door and into the maelstrom of gaudy masks and whirling dancers. He did his best to peer at each one in search of Bryony. What if they'd made it this far, only for him not to recognize her amongst the crowd, or vice versa?

"Lady X!" came the doorman's shout from somewhere behind.

Max whirled around just as the crowd cheered and raised the champagne in toast.

This Lady X could hold no candle to Bryony. The perfect blonde ringlets bouncing behind her extravagant mask were a disappointment.

Once more, he turned his back to the door and

made his way through the throng. If she was in here, he would find her. He would sense her presence the way flowers sought the sun.

The door swung back open. "Lady X!"

The crowd's drunken cheer was deafening.

From his position across the room, Max climbed the first step of a spiral staircase for a better view of the latest newcomer.

Her dress was more than equal to any of the fine ladies present. Translucent gauze over expensive French satin. Puffed sleeves and elbow-length silk gloves. A demi-train with pearl-embroidered lace trim.

None of that interested him.

His heart doubled its beat because it was *her*.

Behind a flamboyant mass of shimmering peacock feathers, her dark brown hair hung down in a curtain, rather than pinned up in carefully curled loops. It was stick-straight and windblown, and the most erotic thing he had seen in his life.

This was his Bryony. He would have recognized her anywhere.

He stepped off the spiral stair and made his way toward her, carving his way through an ocean of dancers as he strode toward his Lady X.

When he reached her, she parted her lips as though about to speak his name.

He greeted her with his mouth instead, telling her with his kiss and his tongue everything he could not say in words.

When at last he pulled away, she twined her arms about his neck. As if her strength came from his. As if they were one.

He would never let her go.

"You came," she whispered, slight hesitation in her voice.

His heart twisted. "Did you doubt me?"

"I was afraid to hope," she admitted. "Shall we dance?"

He placed his untouched glass of champagne on the empty tray of a passing footman and led her onto the dance floor.

Max might not have presented himself before a king or attended any royal balls, but dancing was not reserved for the rich alone. It was something one felt in one's soul.

With Bryony in his arms, it wasn't that the melody didn't matter, but that the music had become part of them. A current, sweeping an endless sea of embracing couples in a seductive rhythm of ebbs and tides.

He held her closer than would otherwise be allowed. What else was the point of a masquerade?

From the stairs, he had already seen couples locked in passionate embraces, as well as the private rooms where one could indulge in more intimate pleasures.

That was not why he was here. He had no wish

to be a despoiler. Bryony was perfect just as she was, and having her in his arms was pleasure enough. Or at least, it would have to be.

His heart thumped. They were in a ballroom filled to capacity and yet privacy was theirs. He could kiss her anytime he wished, and did so again and again in delight. He would never tire of her lips, the sweetness of her taste, her spice.

Being with her was like falling from heaven. Floating through clouds. Lucifer, driven to darkness but tempted by light.

She was his salvation.

Chapter 18

A thrill tingled through Bryony's body at the exhilarating sensation of being in Max's arms.

Somehow, she had recognized him from across the room. Not just because he had come charging toward her with the confidence and arrogance of a king. She'd recognized the curl of his hair, the cut of his jaw, the scent of his skin.

The taste of his kiss.

Being swept into his arms without so much as a how-do-you-do had crowned a fantasy she hadn't realized she'd been keeping. It was as if she had been waiting for that moment her whole life. To be desired so completely that not even a moment could be wasted on words.

Hot, shattering kisses were the only conversation they required. Raw, desperate, honest. A claiming and a submission melded into one.

And now, the night had been set to music.

The effect was magical. Waltzing with Max in this ballroom made her feel as though they had been transported to another world. It was unlike any other dance she'd ever performed.

Perhaps because with him, she wasn't performing. She wanted to be here. Wanted to be with *him*. It felt like all the other dances she'd ever suffered through had been practice for this moment.

She had no need to count the beats in order to match her feet with his. They were of one rhythm. Their bodies cleaved together into a single form as though they shared a single heartbeat. She could not hide her quickness of breath at sharing this masquerade with him.

Her pulse had been skittering with excitement and trepidation since she'd woken up that morning. Consumed with fear that he would not show. Or certainty that he would.

That his first act had been to kiss her in greeting should not have come as a surprise. He was a grantor of wishes. No greater desire filled her heart than for her lips to be tasting his.

For now, she would settle for dancing.

Max's strong arms swirled her through the crowd. "How long has Lambley been doing this?"

"Forever, I think." She let the sound of the orchestra fill her heart. "The masquerades were already an open secret before my come-out."

He stroked her hand with his thumb. "Is it what you expected?"

"More," she answered honestly.

The duke's residence was as enormous as rumored, and filled to capacity. Thrice as many elegant lords and ladies swirled beneath the crystal chandeliers than would fit in Almack's assembly rooms.

Lambley, of course, was instantly identifiable. He never wore a mask. Bryony could not help but wonder if he saw through her peacock feathers to the breathless, giddy woman beneath.

Other guests she recognized because their masks were token at best, or their voice and manner gave them away. A constant hum of chatter buzzed amongst the crowd. Even though neither she nor Max appeared to have any inclination to waste this moment with conversation, a never-ending stream of friendly faces wished them well or raised their glasses in their direction.

At first, she was charmed. The deafening cheer when she'd entered the room had been marvelous. No one knew who she was, yet all were delighted to see her. It seemed fitting that the mood in the ballroom should be festive and celebratory. Heaven knew she herself felt like cheering any time Max pulled her into his arms or lowered his lips to hers.

It took a moment to realize that the random toasts from the crowd did not elicit the same response in Max.

Because she knew him with and without his mask, she sifted through the observable facts to determine why.

In this setting, poets, rakes, and earls treated Max like one of their own. Doe-eyed countesses and expensive demimondaines alike cast flirtatious glances at him from behind their masks. He was not an outcast, but someone to be welcomed with open arms.

And it infuriated him.

Here amidst the gilt and splendor of a ducal estate, he was finally as good as any other... but only because he had hidden his true self.

The masks no longer seemed so charming.

Bryony's heart twisted for the proud, stoic man who continued to lead her about the dance floor. Threading their way through an entire ballroom full of people who would not acknowledge him if they had met anywhere else.

She squeezed his hand in hers as they swirled amongst them.

Snobs and dandies were the ones who should attempt to live up to Max's level, not the other way around.

She tried to imagine what it would be like to waltz with him without masks in a salon as crowded as this.

In what world would it be possible? Would part of him have to crumble inside in order to even try?

Her stomach twisted. He was not the one who ought to change.

Nothing he could do would make him into an idle lordling, and there was no reason to pretend.

If she wished to imagine a life with him, public and unmasked, she would be the one who needed to change. To keep him, she would have to stop trying to drag him into her world and start thinking of a way to better fit into his.

But what did *he* want? What if the answer wasn't her? She knew her faults and her weaknesses. Knew they vastly outnumbered her charms.

"Are you enjoying the dance?" he asked gruffly.

"I hope it doesn't end." She peered up at him. "Unless you're tiring of it?"

He pulled her closer. "A man never tires of holding a beautiful woman in his arms."

A delicious frisson tickled her skin at his words. She wished she could spend every night dancing in his arms. Not as *a* beautiful woman, but as *his*.

Although she had no illusions any man considered her the ideal woman, she hoped she was at least a contender for a small place in his heart.

That *was* why he was here, was it not? Quickly, her mind raced through all the possible options.

Perhaps he had put on a mask and entered a

duke's domain in order for them to share the joy of music together. To dance, heart to heart.

Or perhaps her ruthless, calculating king of the Cloven Hoof was exploiting an obvious weakness in his enemy in order to ensure the odds of receiving the deed to his property tilted in his favor.

If that were true... it would destroy her.

Blast it all. She gazed up at him in irritation and wonder. She was in *love*.

And she desperately wanted him to feel the same.

She held on tight as he spun her through the crowd.

Bryony had funneled every spare penny into commissioning the most extravagant evening gown of her life. Tonight of all nights, she didn't just want to be feminine and attractive. She wanted to attract *Max*. To bewitch him as he had bewitched her.

He was by far the most stunning gentleman in the ballroom. Coal black hair, coal black tailcoat, coal black breeches, coal black boots. Cravat as pristine and white as frost upon an orchid. Blood-red waistcoat, warning that the warrior beneath was not the sort to hide, but to attack. To protect what was his.

It was the boldest color Bryony had seen him in yet. She smiled. He'd worn it for *her*.

And, although he might not realize it, he had also worn it for him.

She tilted her mouth toward his ear. "You look

splendid in crimson."

"Like a robin redbreast?" he answered with a slow smile.

She pressed her body closer. "You could never be anything so dainty as a bird. Your strength is powerful and barely contained. More like a volcano, as hot and unpredictable as lava."

He lowered his lips to her hair. "Then should you be dancing so close to the abyss, fair maiden?"

"I've never felt safer than when in your arms," she answered honestly.

He tipped her chin toward his and kissed her.

Her knees buckled. This was not scalding lava, but brilliant fireworks. The smoke and startling bang only foretold a dazzling display of color and beauty. She could kiss him forever.

He didn't pull his mouth from hers until the music ceased.

It was a short break between sets. Soon, the orchestra would start again. Bryony hesitated. She had never loved dancing as much as when cradled in Max's arms.

But she loved his kisses more.

She peered up at him from behind her mask. "Care to take a turn about the gardens?"

He led her away from the glittering lights and milling bodies to the open terrace doors on the far side of the ballroom.

The air was crisp, but Max would keep her warm.

The night was their blanket. A sliver of moon and a smattering of stars more than enough light for his lips to find hers.

They barely made their way down a gravel path to a secluded stone bench before he pulled her back into his arms. Bryony kissed him with all her love. Kissed him with all her fears. Kissed him with all her hopes, and dreams, and fantasies.

His mouth was hot and dangerous, his hands possessive.

This was no chaste kiss, but a claiming.

He lifted her from the bench to his lap and ran his hands over her form. Memorizing her body. She sank her fingers into his hair, careful not to disturb his mask but mindless of everything else.

Nothing mattered but his kisses.

When his fingers cupped her bosom, she gasped with pleasure and arched into his touch. His hands made her body come alive. Every inch of her tingled. An insatiable pulsation kindled in her core. She wanted more.

Panting, he wrenched his hands from her body and broke the kiss.

When she reached up to pull his lips back to hers, he lifted her from his lap and pulled them both to their feet.

"The orchestra is starting again," he said gruffly.

So it was.

She tried to smile. Dancing came a distant second to kissing in a moonlit garden.

Well, for Bryony. She did not know if Max had stopped the romantic interlude because he was being responsible and gentlemanly or because he did not care to continue.

Perhaps even masks were not enough freedom.

Chapter 19

*A*re you certain this is the right place?" the hackney driver asked.

Max wasn't sure at all.

He stared out the sooty window of the dilapidated hack at the pristine brick façade of Heath Grenville's townhouse.

This was madness.

When Max had first been invited to the "small family gathering," he had been certain he would not attend. Presenting himself as an equal on the most fashionable street in Mayfair defied all logic.

Even the hack driver knew it. The man had picked Max up at his apartment. He knew what kind of home Max had come from.

"It's the right place," Max said as he forced himself out from the safety of the shadows and into the brilliant light of day.

Never had sunlight seemed so ominous.

Dusk wouldn't fall until closer to ten, and the supper invitation was for eight o'clock. Max scowled. He was to arrive in broad daylight, unmasked and exposed. Present himself not to the familiar comfort of a rookery, but to a pristine neighborhood of obvious wealth where each manicured garden was identical to the next.

This was nothing like home.

Street sweepers populated every corner, brushing away the tiniest specks of filth from impeccably clean cobblestones so that elegant passersby should not dirty their hems. For their trouble, the sweepers were rewarded with a coin likely larger than Max had paid his hackney driver.

But money was not the problem.

Nor was he concerned about the chance of gathering dust on his boots as he strode up the tidy walk to the ornate front door. His fingers clenched because he knew not what was on the other side.

Grenvilles, to be sure.

Ideally, only the ones he had met the other day. Yet they had said family and friends. Their friends, not Max's.

His welcome might not last for long.

He lifted his fist to pound upon the door, then caught sight of a freshly polished knocker. Of course. How gauche of him. He lifted the heavy brass ring and gave two curt raps against its base.

The door opened immediately.

It was not Heath Grenville or his wife on the other side. It was not even a disgruntled twelve-year-old in messy plaits and a pinafore.

It was a butler. A real one. The sort who would expect a calling card.

Bloody hell.

They stared at each other in silence.

Max sighed. Nothing for it but to blurt his name and hope the elegant door wasn't slammed in his face.

Before he could do so, the butler stepped aside and swept an arm toward the corridor behind. "This way, Master Gideon."

Max blinked. Gingerly, he crossed the threshold. His heart pounded. Not only had he been invited, special care had been taken to ensure his comfort from the moment his boots reached the front step.

He inclined his head towards the butler. "Thank you."

Did one thank a butler? Max had no idea.

Murmurs of conversation and laughter spilled from an adjoining room.

The butler led him through the corridor to an open doorway and announced his name.

Max braced himself.

No one gasped in alarm or dismay. Instead, a

half dozen familiar faces smiled back at him in welcome.

Heath and his wife. Lord and Lady Wainwright. Mrs. Spaulding, who ran the school for girls and had personally obliterated all dignity from a noble game of cards.

But Max only had eyes for Bryony.

Her eyes shone as he stepped forward to greet her. Her hair was in some sort of a twist. Her gown was a flowing mint silk trimmed with jade satin. But he couldn't tear his gaze from her face.

She looked even more beautiful without the mask.

He tried to keep his breath steady.

"You came," she whispered.

Of course he had. This was where he could find her.

"Mr. Gideon," said the headmistress. "I'd like to introduce you to my husband, Inspector Simon Spaulding."

Max copied Mr. Spaulding's bow as precisely as he could.

"And this is my brother, Carter Winfield," Heath's wife, Nora, gestured to a golden-haired fellow with an ungentlemanly tanned complexion. "He's come all the way from the West Midlands."

"Can't stay long," Mr. Winfield reminded his sister. "Someone's got to take care of the sheep now that you've defected to London."

Max blinked. The sheep?

She sent him the sort of stern frown all sisters seemed to master at a young age. "I thought you hired help. You promised. Next year, I expect you to stay for the Season."

A *sheep* farmer.

Welcome to stay for the Season.

"And next year, my wife will be starring in a new production," Lord Wainwright said with pride. "As usual, my private box is at the disposal of everyone in this room."

An earl's private opera box.

At the disposal of Max and a sheep farmer.

Where on earth was he?

"No doubt by then the girls will have a new Circus Minimus to perform," said the headmistress, eyes shining. She raised a finger toward her brother-in-law. "Sell a few sheep so you can donate to the cause."

Max turned his baffled gaze toward Bryony.

"Circus Minimus is an acrobatic charity performance the students put on to raise funds for their school," she whispered. "A few of them are almost as good at somersaults and flips as my sister."

Max swung his gaze back to the headmistress. This he would have to see.

The thought of future plans rooted him in place.

Would he honestly be attending a charity performance of any kind? Did he truly pretend that he was penciling in to his agenda a date to avail himself of an earl's private opera box?

Never before had such outlandish notions crossed his mind.

Now he found himself wanting to believe in their possibility more than anything. Not to hear the famed soprano, or even to witness highflying school-girls, but the dizzying idea that Bryony could still be in his life after the month was through.

Even if it meant sitting in the back row watching her enjoy the festivities with her new husband. By next Season, she would be wed.

His stomach clenched. The idea of her spending so much as a single night with anyone else made him nauseous. Not just with jealousy, but a yawning sense of loss. Of fear. Of denial.

He *loved* her, damn it all.

She was his world. Or at least, he would like her to be. But he didn't see how.

As strange and disparate as her family was, as her siblings might be, they had given him no indica-tion that they considered him anything more than a friend of the family. Even that much was a significant level of polite condescension. Far more than he would have hoped for.

But he knew where the line was drawn.

No matter how much he believed in the honest desire in Bryony's kisses, her future husband was not hers to choose. Her parents would select a gentleman perfect for her. Someone who wasn't Max.

"Going foxing at Underhill's hunting cabin next week?" Lord Wainwright asked the other men.

Heath Grenville shook his head. "I've a situation to resolve with a client."

"And a new exhibition to finalize," his wife added with a proud smile. "'Romanticism in Modern Art' will be the gallery's finest collection to date."

Their love was obvious.

Max tamped down his envy.

He should not be surprised Grenville had managed to marry as he wished. He was the son. A grown man, a future baron, fixer of Society's greatest scandals. If anyone could manage to wed a commoner without facing social disaster, it would be a man in Heath Grenville's position.

Bryony, on the other hand, was the youngest girl. Her eldest sister had married an earl. No doubt her parents believed she could improve upon that feat.

The middle sister might be untitled, but he supposed a Bow Street Runner caused the family no shame. Inspectors like him were honest and smart, swift and capable. The sort of man lords and ladies would call to fix their wrongs. Someone whose presence improved their lives.

And then there was Max. He did not cause the same effect. An attachment to him would sully Bryony's name, rather than honor it. That wasn't something he would voluntarily put her through. No matter how much he might wish their future could be otherwise.

Besides, he would have to join the queue of admirers. His lips curled. Even his sister had managed to propose marriage to Bryony before Max could.

Not that she was likely to take a proposal from him any more seriously than she had taken the joking one from his sister.

How could he ask her to submit to a life of not fitting in, when he knew from first-hand experience how much that hurt?

"I like your family," he murmured to Bryony.

Her eyes twinkled. "They're perfect, aren't they?"

Someone was. He wished he could kiss her.

In one costume or another, she always managed to straddle the line between what was accepted in her society and a secret life filled with what was not. She was a walking contradiction and he loved her for it. Baron's daughter by day, gaming hell financier by night. He could not help but admire her.

"This is a very unconventional gathering," he murmured to Bryony.

Her grin was instantaneous. "Have I somehow given you the misconception that I am a conventional lady?"

His breath caught. No, she hadn't. And he adored her for it.

Two months ago, he would never have believed his future would include long nights in his office managing a gaming hell with an equally managing female. He would never have dreamed of meeting her for ices, paying a social call to a girls' school, or dancing beneath countless chandeliers at a masquerade.

None of that had taken half as much courage as presenting himself on the doorstep tonight. Those stolen moments had been fantasy. He had longed for the possibility of something more. Had not dared to believe it possible, until now.

This was reality. And it was... Splendid.

He brushed the back of his fingers against Bryony's hand. She smiled up at him from beneath her lashes. He clenched his jaw in determination.

If he could survive an evening in a neighborhood this lofty, with companions this diverse, then he could survive another. And another. And another.

Perhaps even a lifetime of such evenings. Was it too much to hope? He would prove it to himself tonight, and then he would prove it to Bryony.

Maybe they really could make a future together.

Chapter 20

*B*ryony couldn't stop smiling. She was overjoyed Max had chosen to accept her brother's invitation, despite his obvious initial reservations.

She understood Max's reticence. In other circumstances, his caution would have been sound. He would soon learn to consider her siblings' homes a safe place. A chance to pass a quiet evening with loved ones without their parents present to scold or pass judgment.

In fact, this was the perfect opportunity for Max to discover how lovable her siblings were. And for her extended family to see for themselves how wonderful he was.

And, *oh*, was he wonderful, inside and out. She slid another look his way. Tonight he was positively resplendent.

He wore perfectly polished Hessians, along with black breeches and a tailcoat that perfectly emphasized his powerful frame. His cravat was as white and crisp and effusive as that of any London gentleman. Her pulse quickened.

Jaw, only slightly shadowed. Thick black hair curling to his neck unrepentantly. Bold waistcoat as bright orange as flame, like the gaming hell he presided over, like the demon everyone believed him to be.

His armor didn't fool her. She knew the truth of the man inside. Yes, he was unquestionably arrogant and ruthless and impossible. Of this, she was in full agreement. But he was also gentle and caring. Behind a dark and guarded exterior, shimmered the soul of a poet.

Was it any wonder she loved him?

"When does supper start?" he growled into her ear.

Bryony grinned. "When we're called to the table. Soon, I promise."

She wished she could take his hand and place it to her cheek.

He narrowed his eyes. "Is this the sort of soirée where gentlemen separate from the ladies after dinner in order to consume inadvisable quantities of port without being forced by proximity to share the spoils with women?"

She gave a careless shrug. "You may do so if you choose, but I cannot promise the ladies will leave anything but crumbs once the dessert trays arrive from the kitchen."

"What are the chances of currant biscuits?" he asked hopefully, his eyes as guileless and eager as a child.

"Low, I'm afraid," she said sorrowfully. "I fear Heath will try to impress us with multi-layer torts and sugar-crystaled brûlée. Will you be able to make do?"

He lifted his nose. "I will suffer in silence."

She grinned back at him. "I did not realize you were addicted to currant biscuits."

"I haven't had one in ages," he admitted. "My mother would make them for special occasions, and for a while my sister did the same. These days, she hasn't time."

Bryony nodded. She was working on that.

"Why don't you bake the biscuits yourself?" she teased.

"I have," he said instantly. "To my immense consternation, it turns out they taste much better when shared with others."

Her heart flipped.

In that moment, Bryony vowed her greatest achievement would be the day she baked him his favorite biscuits and they shared them together, warm and fresh from the oven.

Perhaps they could make it a tradition of their own.

She leaned toward him. "I was thinking—"

A motion in the corridor caught her eye.

Her stomach sank.

It was not a footman calling them to supper, but the butler arriving with an unexpected guest.

"Lady Grenville," he announced calmly, as if the cozy romantic evening Bryony had planned was not about to be shattered.

"Mother." Heath greeted her with equanimity. "What a surprise. I thought you were booked elsewhere tonight."

"Lady Febland came down with the ague." Mother cast her sharp gaze about the room, taking each face in turn.

Heath was dapper as ever, of course. His wife Nora sweet and elegant. Nor would one know by looking at Carter that he was more at home on a farm than in a ballroom. To anyone's eyes, he was dressed to perfection. Mother's gaze did not linger there.

As always, Camellia and her husband looked every inch the earl and countess that they were. Wainwright's pockets were bottomless, and his favorite hobby was spoiling his wife.

True, Dahlia and Simon weren't quite as wealthy. Every spare crown went toward the school whenever possible. But she had been born a Grenville, and never failed to acquit herself prettily.

Simon was born out of wedlock, but to a titled father. She granted even him a tight smile.

And then there was Bryony.

Tonight, she had dressed with extra care. Even though Max had claimed he would not be in attendance, her heart had not ceased to hope. She had even submitted to curling tongs in order to ensure she presented herself as attractively as possible. Mother had likely never seen her youngest child try so hard to make herself beautiful. The side-curls alone would win Bryony a spot in her mother's good graces for at least the rest of the week.

But then, inevitably, dreadfully, Mother's hawkish gaze alighted on Max.

Bryony's heart sank.

It was obvious in an instant that his painstakingly shined boots, exquisitely tailored waistcoat, and carefully tied cravat did not signify in the least.

Mother's eyes were focused with crystal sharpness on the stubble at his jaw, the too-long curl of his hair, the shocking bronze of his skin.

Before Bryony could say a word, Heath jumped in with the introductions. "Mr. Gideon, it is my honor to introduce my mother, Lady Grenville. Mother, this is my esteemed and invited guest, Mr. Maxwell Gideon."

The gambit would not work.

Mother was no stranger to scandal columns. The name was immediately recognizable. A gambling den like the Cloven Hoof was not something she wished associated with any of her children.

She made no attempt to hide the horror in her voice or the disgusted wrinkle of her nose. "What is *he* doing here?"

Heath tried again. "Mr. Gideon is—"

But Mother had already analyzed the situation and determined the only probable reason a man like him would be present, and standing so close to Bryony.

"Get out," she said coldly, advancing on him like a fishwife chasing off a stray mutt. "This is a family gathering. Stay away from my daughter. You must know you are not worthy of speaking to her."

The stoic blankness of Max's expression broke Bryony's heart.

He was wrapping himself in all the arrogance, and pride, and disinterest he could muster, to protect himself from hurt. But it was too late. The sword had already struck true.

"Mother, stop." Bryony stepped between them, praying there was some way to diffuse the horrible situation before her fragile connection with Max was gone forever. "He is a good man. A guest in this home."

"A mongrel," Mother corrected, her hands shaking in anger. "I won't allow such a creature near my daughter."

"He's not a *thing*," Bryony burst out in fury. "He

is the sweetest, smartest, most capable person I know, and I am proud to say that I—"

"Stop," Max said quietly. "This is the only mother you'll ever have, and she is right to want what is best for her daughter. We both know that's not me."

He made the prettiest bow Bryony had ever seen, and walked out into the night with his head held high, leaving only his memory behind.

Chapter 21

*A*fter a fitful night, Bryony awoke long before her parents and made her way out the front door with a package beneath her arm. She took not a hackney, but the family coach.

Her errands today would be performed as Bryony, not Basil Q. Jones. She was done hiding. Now and forever.

She allowed a footman to lift first her, then her package, into the coach and send her on her way.

No one asked where she was going. They never did.

She gave the driver a direction and settled back on the squab.

Her heart beat as ferociously as thunder. It had not calmed for even a moment since her mother's cruel words had cut Max so deeply and ruined the bond that Bryony had come to cherish.

No doubt, the evening had gone exactly as he feared.

She could not blame him or his sister for despising the upper classes. Purists like her mother didn't seem like "betters" at all.

Bryony clenched her fingers at the injustice. Max had allowed her into his club, invited her into his home. She would not allow anyone to shut him out now.

Not even her mother.

But the damage was done. If he had been uncertain before whether there could be any attachment between them, Mother had put such doubts to rest.

Her expectations for Bryony and her future could not have been clearer. Max was not a part of it. Bryony's own wishes did not signify. She was a baron's daughter and would do as instructed.

Not today.

Gooseflesh danced across her skin. If she never saw Max again, she could not blame him. Anyone could understand him never again wishing to step foot anywhere he might cross paths with a Grenville.

But the future was outside her control. What mattered most was what action she could take right now. If one witnessed a hurt, a lack, a need, it was one's duty not to stand idle and allow cruelty to prevail. Bryony's parents had the power to deny any suitor they wished. There was no need to humiliate

Max in front of the entire family.

More than that, *Max* was now family. *Frances* was now family. Bryony intended to treat them like it.

Even if they would never know.

She could not undo Mother's hurtful words to Max, and was still frantically running through hypotheses as to whether the bridge that had been broken could be rebuilt. She hoped so. Max was too important to lose.

The situation with Frances, however, was easier to resolve. If there was one thing Bryony understood even better than numbers, it was helping sisters. She'd had a lifetime of practice.

"This is it," said the driver as he pulled the horses to a stop. "Shall I come in with you?"

"No need. Stay here with the horses." Bryony accepted his hand to alight from the carriage and hefted her carefully wrapped parcel in her arms.

Today was the day.

It was a typical London morning. Cold and gray and rainy. Perfect for what she was about to do.

She made her way into the pawn shop and set her violin case upon the counter.

"Miss Grenville," said the pawnbroker with a smile. "An age since I seen you last."

Bryony nodded. This was where she had sold her prized possessions to fund that first nest egg that allowed the creation of Basil Q. Jones, and later led her to Max's door. A lifetime ago.

For the past few years, she hadn't needed to pawn anything of value. Her investments had been wildly profitable. Enough so to allow her to purchase outright the very property upon which the Cloven Hoof stood.

But every penny had gone to purchasing that deed. Last month's rent, to the gown she'd worn to the masquerade. She needed more. A lot more. Enough to cover a year or two's salary.

She unwrapped the linen and opened the case. "What will you give me?"

"Let's see what we have." He lifted his quizzing glass from the counter before inspecting Bryony's violin.

The color drained from his face. He turned to her with eyes wide with shock.

"A Stradivarius?" he breathed in awe and disbelief. "You cannot be serious."

She pulled a sheaf of papers from beneath her cloak and laid them on the counter. "Proof of provenance. You will have no trouble earning back every pound you give me, and I expect a fair amount."

He was barely listening, so enraptured was he in inspecting every swirl and key, every string and hollow.

Mother would not forgive Bryony for this act of defiance.

Bryony pressed her lips together. The few compliments Mother had ever spoken were all related to Bryony's prowess with an instrument. *This* instrument. Although Mother had not been the one to purchase the violin, she had been the brains and the impetus behind the Grenville family musicales.

Her throat pricked. Soon the violin would be gone.

Not only was her gift with music the primary reason for the acceptance of a misfit like Bryony in High Society, the runaway success of the family musicales was what had made a low-ranking baroness like her mother into a reigning queen of London.

The Grenvilles were famous because of their music.

Parliament might bring lords to London each Season, but the Grenville musicales brought everyone else. Seating was limited, invitations exclusive. A spectacle rumored not to be missed.

Without the musicales, Bryony was no one. And neither was her mother.

At last, the pawnbroker murmured a number.

"Double it," she replied without hesitation.

He glanced up from the violin in pique. "Now, look here, miss. I'm a working man. Ye can't possibly expect..."

Whatever was written on Bryony's expression at that moment must have indicated she very much expected negotiations to go her way.

"One and a half," he hedged.

"Double," Bryony said again. The numbers were in her favor.

This was more than a couple years' salary. It was food, it was clothes, it was lodging. It would mean freedom.

"I'm starting to dislike you," the pawnbroker muttered as he scratched out an IOU.

"Everyone eventually does," Bryony said cheerfully as she pocketed the slip of parchment. "When will the funds be in my account?"

"Dusk, if not sooner." He ran a longing finger over the violin. "I believe I'll close early today."

"Enjoy." Bryony turned and walked away.

Arms now empty, she made her way back to the family coach feeling like she'd left part of her soul behind. A hollowness carved from her heart where music once used to be.

She motioned to the driver.

This was it. The point of no return. By driving away and leaving her violin behind, she had changed her life forever.

No, not only her own.

As soon as her mother discovered this treachery, her disappointment would be all encompassing. Rather like how Bryony had felt watching vitriol spew from her mother's mouth with the sole aim of hurting the man Bryony loved.

Her chest shuddered.

Selling her Stradivarius meant choosing between one family and another. It was a private decision. Neither Max nor his sister need learn of the sacrifice. Bryony had no expectation of glory. Only a desire to protect those she loved. Those she could.

Max's business would be fine. She had seen to that. And now, she would see to Frances.

As soon as she was once again seated before her writing desk, she chose her finest stationery and began to pen instructions to her private bank.

As always, the money would arrive at the St. Giles School for Girls as a pseudonymous donation.

This time, however, the funds came with conditions. They could only be used for the hiring, salary, and well-being of a new teacher with a very specific set of expertise.

"Horace B. Puscat" might even name a suggestion.

Chapter 22

*M*ax was at his dining room table leafing through an old journal when the knock came upon his door. He pretended not to hear it.

Frances would not have knocked, but barged right in. And he was not expecting any visitors. Even *he* shouldn't have been at home. The Cloven Hoof needed him. But after last night's disastrous attempt to attend Heath Grenville's dinner party as some sort of equal, Max's desire to be around people had waned significantly.

He would not soon forget Lady Grenville's disgust at his presence. His gut clenched. Her rebuke had been harsh, but honest. She had said nothing that Max did not already know. He was not the one for Bryony. He never would be.

Which was exactly why he was in no mood for company.

The racket came again, banging harder this time.

He tried to ignore it. There were sums to... damn it, he had no idea what page he was on.

The knocking grew in volume and urgency.

Clenching his jaw, Max slammed his journal shut and stalked over to the entrance. He flung open the door in fury.

Bryony stood on the other side with a lumpy satchel cradled in one arm and a baking pan clutched in the other hand. "Hungry?"

He was indeed.

A hunger too deep and too visceral to name filled him every time he looked at her, even when she only lived in his memory.

But he did not move out of the way.

"Why are you here?" he asked coldly. No good could come of this for either of them. "Your mother's wishes were clear enough."

"And I am clearly not my mother," Bryony rejoined. "She would forbid my hair from growing straight if she could."

Perhaps so. Forbidding her daughter from seeing Max was far more practical than straight hair.

"Are you going to let me in?" Bryony asked.

He curled his lip. "No."

She used the back of the heavy baking pan to nudge him aside and squeezed through anyway. "I must borrow your kitchen."

He followed right behind her. "Is something wrong with yours?"

"Too much smoke," she said. "I nearly burned it down."

He choked. "Bryony—"

She swung the satchel and the baking pan atop the small table and glanced about for a tinderbox.

"Is there anything I should know about your oven before I begin?" she asked.

"Fire is hot?" he answered. "I only have one flat. Please don't burn it down."

"So noted." She untied her satchel and placed its contents beside the pan. Flour, sugar, butter, eggs, currants.

"You're baking biscuits?" he asked in disbelief.

"I'm attempting to," she clarified. "I've been practicing all morning and the last batch didn't break any teeth."

She rummaged about for a bowl and began combining ingredients without any regard for proper order or quantity.

"Have you ever baked anything before?" he asked suspiciously.

"I just told you." She stirred the contents of the bowl with a long wooden spoon. "I've been practicing all morning."

He watched, speechless.

Once she managed to mash the ingredients together into somewhat cohesive lumps, she dropped spoonfuls of batter onto her baking pan and placed it in his oven.

"There," she said with pride. "It probably won't burn down."

It probably also wouldn't be edible.

But that wasn't the point. Max's chest warmed. She could have purchased currant biscuits at a bakery or the market. Instead, she'd wanted to make them for him herself. Because he'd said he liked them. Because she wanted to please him.

"You don't have to do this," he said softly.

"Trust me," she said. "You'll wish I hadn't. I'll expect you to eat them anyway."

His lips twitched. "They are already my favorite."

Bryony ran an idle fingertip along the edge of the mixing bowl, then lifted her gaze to his. "I'm terrible at a lot of things. I'm terrible at sewing. I'm terrible at cooking."

She seemed to be waiting for a reply.

"I am... better than you at both those things," he admitted. "But I'm not looking for a tailor or a chef."

She appeared to think this over.

"I come from a mostly perfect family. That is, my siblings and their spouses are the finest people I know." She winced. "My parents, on the other hand..."

"...are parents," he finished for her. "They want

what is best for you."

"Even if I don't agree on what that might be,"
Bryony said with a sigh. "But who can blame them?
I'm stubborn and impulsive—"

"Smart and beautiful," he interrupted.

"—independent and mannish—"

"Kindhearted and talented," he said firmly.

"—more interested in numbers than fashion—"

He grabbed her wrists and pulled her to him.
"You're perfect exactly as you are. What is the point
of this line of talk?"

"That I'm not better than you." Her voice was ur-
gent. "My mother is wrong. You are a person anyone
would wish to be like. I'm not too good for you.
You're too good for me."

His throat was suddenly tight. "Poppycock.
You're just trying to get me to kiss you."

She peered up at him through her lashes. "Is it
working?"

In reply, he slanted his mouth over hers.

She was indeed a brilliant, headstrong, fascinating, maddening creature. She was exactly what he
needed.

Her mother's bluntness might have dashed any
foolish hopes for a future together, but she had done
nothing to quench Max's desire for having Bryony
right now.

She was more than a desire. She was an addic-
tion.

That was why he had to stop kissing her, no matter how sweet her lips. He couldn't keep losing himself in the moment when this moment was all that they had. He knew better. And yet he could not tear his lips from hers.

She tasted like spun sugar and possibility. Rainbows after a summer storm.

Every kiss ripped another crack in the stone encasing his heart. If he did not stop soon, all his defenses would crumble away.

He did not dare take such a risk when he already knew the outcome.

Yet when he was with her, logic no longer prevailed. The rhythm of his pulse made him pull her ever closer. It was a dance. A melody. The yearning in his heart made him deepen every kiss. The throbbing of his—

Smoke. Something smelled like smoke.

Bryony tore her mouth from his with a horrified gasp. "The biscuits are on fire!"

Not yet, but they would be soon if Max did not take immediate action to rectify the situation.

He wrapped the closest washrag about his hand and pulled the baking pan from the fire.

Twelve generously toasted lumps greeted them.

Bryony's eyes shimmered.

"I practiced all morning," she whispered brokenly. "I wanted them to be perfect. For you. I wanted to *be* perfect, just this once."

"You are." He yanked her back into his embrace. "You always have been."

This kiss was different. More savage. More vulnerable.

He loved that she'd baked him a dozen burnt biscuits. He loved her for being her. For coming to call when she should not. For breaking into his club when she should not. For being in his arms when she should not.

She had tried her damnedest to make room for him in her world and was hoping he could offer her a tiny slice of his.

What the daft woman didn't realize was that she already *was* his world. He couldn't make a place for her when she was already everything that mattered.

He hoisted her up onto the edge of the table, so she would not have to stay on her toes to kiss him. His hips nestled perfectly between her thighs. The battle was over. He was helpless to resist her.

She was all he needed.

He returned his attentions to kissing her. He had been afraid the opportunity wouldn't arise again. That he had lost her for good.

"Thank you for the biscuits," he said between kisses.

"You haven't tried them," she murmured and licked the corner of his mouth.

"I'd like to taste something sweeter." He cupped his hands about her arse and pulled her close. "*You.*"

"I'm here," she whispered. "Show me."

Those were the words Max had longed to hear.

Everything else he wanted to tell her, he could say with his mouth another way.

He ran his hands up the curve of her hips to her rib cage. She had the body of a siren. If she was singing him to his death, so be it.

Gently, he cupped her breasts. She immediately leaned into his touch.

"I was hoping you'd do that again," she whispered. "I haven't stopped thinking about your hands on my body since that night."

Neither had he. It was time to give her something more to think about.

He rubbed a finger over the hardened peaks beneath her bodice, then tugged the thin fabric down to expose her breasts. Her bare nipple between his fingers was enough to turn him hard as stone.

He wanted her to know the pleasure he could bring. What they could do together. He lowered his lips to her naked flesh and took her breast in his mouth.

She gasped and arched into him, clutching the back of his collar as if to keep him close. He wasn't going anywhere.

As he suckled her nipple, he lifted the hems of her gown and shift and slipped his hand beneath. She was hot and wet and ready for his touch.

She would be his undoing.

Yet he couldn't stop.

He rubbed in lazy circles, coaxing, teasing. When her breath quickened and her pulse turned staccato, he pushed her legs apart and placed his tongue where his fingers had been to taste her sweetness.

She gave a little moan of pleasure. He slid his hands up her inner thighs and held on as she arched into him, trembling with each lick.

He told her with his tongue the things he couldn't say with his mouth. How much she meant. How he longed to please her. That his world was a brighter place with her in it.

She let out a sudden gasp. Her legs clamped tight about him, convulsing in delicious rhythm with the heat of her climax.

When the spasms ceased, he lifted his head from beneath her skirts and arranged them back over her trembling legs.

"Biscuit?" he enquired innocently.

"Bedchamber," she ordered as she wrapped her legs about his hips and held on tight. "*Now.*"

Chapter 23

*A*re you certain this is what you want?" Max asked.

Bryony cupped her hands to his jaw and kissed him as an answer.

Of course she was certain. He was everything she could want. How could he still doubt? The intimacy of what they had just shared proved that any other future paled compared to a life with him. They belonged together.

He lay her in the center of his bed as if she were a delicate flower who could be swept away at any moment by a gust of wind.

She was not so fragile.

His dark eyes did not waver, his voice as intense as his gaze. "I need you to be sure."

"I'm sure." She held out her arms for him to join

her and reveled in the weight and heat of his body.
This was what she had been waiting for.

She had been sure for weeks. She had been sure
when she gifted him her hideous pillow, when she
gushed about him to her siblings and begged for
them to meet, when she had serenaded him with her
violin in his office, when she had presented herself
on his doorstep with a baking pan and a bag of currants.

She had never been surer about anything in her
life.

He was the one.

Her heart raced at the delicious prospect of making love to him. Of giving themselves to each other
completely, now and forever.

His kisses were both possessive and tender. As
though he wished to claim her, to conquer, and to
keep her safe. As if by kissing him in return, she too
was doing the claiming and the conquering, making
him hers.

When he moved to sit up, she followed. Laughing
between kisses as they tried to shuck their boots and
vestments and unmentionables without lifting their
lips from each other.

The sight of Max nude put every Grecian statute
to shame. He was no boy, no cherubic angel, but a
man. *Her* man.

She hoped he found her body as pleasing. She

suddenly felt small and pale and naked. Not a goddess, but a waif. Perhaps a disappointment.

The hunger in his eyes told a different story.

"I love that big, beautiful brain of yours," he murmured as he kissed her temple. "Turn it off. No mathematics allowed in the bedchamber."

She grinned despite herself. "What would you have me do instead?"

"Enjoy," he answered simply. "Close your eyes. Feel the music."

She allowed her lashes to flutter closed and was rewarded with a kiss so deep she felt it in her very soul.

When at last he lifted his mouth from hers, he immediately replaced it elsewhere on her body. Licking. Kissing. Suckling.

With her eyes closed, she had no way to know where his lips would brush next. Perhaps her breasts. Perhaps a nipple. Perhaps her stomach. Perhaps much lower.

The delicious not-knowing heightened her senses. Every inch of her body felt alive, crackling with awareness.

This was his serenade, she realized. Every kiss was music, every pleasurable lick a soaring melody.

When he returned his mouth between her legs to the place he had tasted before, her body instantly quickened, welcoming the growing crescendo within. She tried to wait. To dance together. Just when she thought she couldn't hold it back any longer, he lifted his mouth from her legs. He settled his hips against hers instead, his shaft hot and thick between them.

"This may hurt." His eyes begged forgiveness. "I shall make it as good as I can."

There was no need for forgiveness. She'd been dreaming of this moment for too long. Yearning to join him as one.

She wrapped her legs about his hips.

"I'm yours," she whispered. "I'm ready."

He covered her mouth with his as he entered her, swallowing her gasp, sweetening the pain. Soon, there was only a fullness inside her, quickly replaced by pleasure as he began to rock his hips.

It was better than she'd dreamed. Everything she had hoped. A symphony unlike any other. They were finally dancing.

When he slid his hand between them to coax the music even higher, this time, she could no longer hold the crescendo back.

"Max," she gasped. "I think you're going to make me—"

"Thank God," he muttered, pumping faster in time with her body's spasms and then quickly jerking free to bury his hips against the blanket. Without lifting his face from the mattress, he swung a powerful arm over her naked form and pulled her close.

She nestled into his warmth with a sigh of contentment. The muscles between her thighs still gave the occasional twitch of pleasure, her mind still flooded with pleasurable sensations.

"Biscuit?" she whispered into his hair.

"Later." He pulled her tight into his embrace, locking both strong arms about her as if he would never let her go.

Chapter 24

*T*he following evening, Bryony felt almost silly donning her costume of trousers and tailcoat to meet Max at the Cloven Hoof.

Now that they'd seen each other with no clothes at all, she rather wished all their encounters could be conducted in such a manner.

Her stomach fluttered whenever she remembered the events of the previous day. All she could think about was what they had done in the kitchen, and in his bedchamber. She hoped every meal they shared from now on would detour just as deliciously.

As the hackney cab carried her closer to Max, she realized she had left with her head so high in the clouds, they had failed to discuss what happened next. Obviously she would marry him, but it wouldn't hurt to iron out a few of the details.

She grinned to herself as she alighted from the hack and made her way to the back door of the Cloven Hoof. Perhaps they would start a new journal together. One that chronicled their shared life outside of the club.

She reached in her coat pocket for the key.

The door was unlocked. Max stood there waiting, just inside the shadowed corridor. His arms folded over his chest.

Bryony's elation turned to panic. He didn't look like a man in love. He looked like a man who wished to throttle her.

"What is it?" she asked.

He continued to block the entrance. "Frances has a new post. She's not a seamstress anymore. She's been offered better housing and three times the salary to become an instructor at a boarding school."

"Isn't that good news?" Bryony stammered, her skin turning clammy.

"Coincidental, wouldn't you say?" His dark eyes glittered at her from the shadows. "Why, isn't the St. Giles School for Girls the same charity your sister founded?"

"It's a growing school," Bryony managed. "They need all the help they can get."

"All your help, you mean." He still hadn't moved an inch. "It seems there was an anonymous donation with very specific conditions."

Bryony's hackles began to rise. How dare he try to make her feel bad for doing something good? His sister deserved every opportunity, no matter how it came about.

"You're her brother," she snapped. "I thought you'd be happy."

His voice was cold. "I'm thrilled for Fran. But I'm disappointed for us."

She had no idea what he was talking about. "There's nothing wrong with accepting help. You yourself tried to—"

"That's right," he said harshly. "I myself tried to help my sister. Rescuing her is something I have been trying to do my entire life, and you went around behind my back—behind both our backs—without so much as talking it over."

Bryony frowned. "It was just a donation. I've given hundreds. I don't need your permission to—"

"It is not a matter of permission," he enunciated in anger. "You took me out of the equation altogether. Robbed me of the courtesy of being a team."

Her body froze in place. He was right. She had done that.

"Manipulating from on high isn't treating some-one like family," he said, eyes flashing. "It proves you weren't thinking about us at all. Another day of Miss Grenville doing whatever she wants, because she can. Just like all the other debutantes and ladies of your set."

He was right. She *hadn't* thought.

"It's not just that you presume to know how to run our lives better than those of us who must actually live them," he continued inexorably. "It's that you come into my club, into my home, into my bed. And you don't even bother to talk to me about the things I care about most."

Her legs trembled.

"I am not your plaything," he said quietly. "Frances and I are not your dolls, awaiting puppet-mastery. We are people, too. I thought you knew that."

Hot pinpricks seared the back of her throat and stung her eyes. Of course she had disappointed him. She disappointed everyone. And she was exactly as he painted her.

Her breaths were shallow.

Even when she tried to do the right thing, she ended up hurting those she loved.

"It wasn't my intention," she whispered. "I didn't mean—"

Max cast her a flat look. "You are the smartest person I know. When have you ever done something you didn't mean? If you had spared a single thought, paused to consider whether Frances would wish to determine the course of her life on her own, you might have concluded that these are the sorts of things one does *with* someone, not against their knowledge."

She hung her head. His conclusion was incontrovertible.

"I cannot believe you didn't take the brief moment it would have required to think things through. After everything. After us." He dropped his arms to his sides as if defeated. "You just acted. On what *you* wanted, *you* felt, *you* decided."

"I thought it was the right thing," she whispered.

"Life isn't always a matter of being right. It's about making other people feel like they matter." His eyes were haunted. "The worst thing you can do to someone who has never had anything, is to take away their power to choose for themselves."

Bryony sucked in a shuddering breath at those words. They hurt because they were true. She wanted to marry this man, to live in bliss forever, yet when given the opportunity to treat him like a partner, she had cut him out instead.

Of course he would be hurt.

He had spent his life trying to help his sister. She and Max might have pooled their resources, found a way to offer Frances an option that allowed her to choose her destiny for herself.

But that was not the path Bryony had taken.

Instead, she was standing outside a gaming hell staring up at the man she loved. The man she had hurt. The man who blocked the entrance. She had lost her right to be let in. *Blackballed.*

As she deserved.

Her grand sacrifice had been for nothing. All she'd wanted to do was show her love. She had ended up alone, facing unending repercussions. By selling her violin, she had also lost her right to be part of her own family. Now she'd alienated Max, too.

She fought back tears. They solved nothing. She had gotten so close to everything she had always wanted. The confidence to just be herself and the great fortune to find someone who liked her for her differences, rather than despite them. And it was all falling apart. She couldn't lose him. Now that they'd finally found love.

"I'm sorry," she whispered. "In the future—"

"We don't have to worry about the future," he said. "It is no business of mine what happens when Lord Moneybreeches puts a ring on your finger and allows you to rule over his household however you wish. You'll be good at it. You've proven that."

Lord Moneybreeches.

Cold fingers of ice snaked through Bryony's chest and encased her heart in its grip. Even after making love, Max still intended their paths to diverge.

Her pulse fluttered in horror.

Belatedly, she realized he had never made a single verbal commitment beyond granting her a month to shadow his club. Not even yesterday, when they had joined bodies. She closed her eyes as the available facts clarified to terrible precision.

His repeated *Are you sure this is what you want?* was because he was offering her ruin, not marriage.

Not out of heartlessness, she realized. He was being logical. She should have done the same.

Even if he would have presented himself to her father, Bryony would not have been granted permission to marry him. If they made the attempt regardless, her parents would protest at the first banns and lock her straight into a nunnery. Or a madhouse.

She was not destined to live happily ever after with Max. The only place such a fantasy had seemed possible was inside her own mind.

Those were the facts.

He wasn't breaking off a commitment. She'd failed to make one in the first place.

"You're right," she said briskly, blinking as fast as possible to keep the tears at bay. "Managing Lord Moneybreeches's life will keep me busy. Nonetheless, I am sorry to have disappointed you. I thought you would know my heart by now."

His gaze was shuttered. "I guess I wanted you to be someone you're not."

"Me too," she whispered, then turned and walked away.

When she got home, she would put away her top hat and her breeches and her tailcoat. It was past time to return to the life of a debutante in search of a lord. Accept the cage she was meant to live in. The role Society expected of her.

She had no other cards to play.

Chapter 25

*M*ax closed the door and walked back to his office on wooden legs.

Was he disappointed with the realization that Bryony might like his club, might like his body, might like his mind, but it still hadn't occurred to her to think of them as a team?

Yes. That would always hurt.

But it wasn't her fault.

He was the one who should have known better from the start. There had been nothing but signs. He had been shown his whole life that his needs didn't matter as much as others'. His wants were unimportant. His feelings, not a consideration.

She had been the first person to make him believe it wasn't true. That his desires could hold equal importance. That his experience was just as valid.

Clearly, he was not as intelligent as he had led himself to believe.

That her family had forbidden the match anyway was just as well. Max didn't want a supplicant's relationship with Bryony. He wanted everything. Her heart. Her respect. Her soul.

After all, that's what she had taken from him.

He slumped back in his chair and gazed sullenly at his empty office. He hated how silent it was. Hated that he had let down his guard and changed what he expected from the world.

Without her, it was like each day dawned without music or color.

Before he'd met her, he had preferred it that way. Convinced himself gray and black and shadows were what he deserved. What he needed.

She had given him another perspective. A brighter one, filled with melody and laughter.

And now there was nothing.

He propped his elbows atop his desk and buried his face in his hands. His temples pounded. He hated to lose her. His heart ached as though it had been squeezed by rough hands and wrung dry.

At least he still ran the Cloven Hoof. That was something, was it not? He lifted his head and stared at the empty settee across the room.

Frances was right. The club wasn't Max's anymore. In this, at least, he and Bryony had been partners. Every room, every table, every bottle of wine now reminded him of her.

He slapped open his agenda and glared at the week's entry.

Three more days before she was meant to decide what to do with the deed. Sell the property to him? Or keep it for herself?

He might be angry and he might be hurt. Above all, frustrated that even if they hadn't argued, they still couldn't be together. Her mother was only echoing the thoughts of all their peers.

But when it came to business, he knew Bryony well.

This past month, she had worked as hard as he had to optimize and improve every aspect of the Cloven Hoof.

He did not want her to sell the property due to emotional manipulation. She had earned her stake. Bought the land out from under him before he'd been clever enough to do so himself.

She was the smartest person he had ever met. Her many feats weren't impressive merely because she was a woman, or even in spite of it. She was competent and driven. She deserved everything she had achieved. Deserved every scrap of success she had earned for herself despite everyone telling her she could not.

Max knew what that was like. He would not perpetuate the problem. Not when it was in his power to be different.

He loved her too much.

Hands shaking, he slid a fresh sheet of parchment before him and dipped his quill in the ink. If he wished to argue that he and Frances deserved an opportunity to determine their own fates, so did Bryony.

He bent his head over the paper and began to write.

Even though it meant letting go of his own dreams for the future of the Cloven Hoof, even though this act did not change the future for himself and Bryony, Max quickly drafted a document formally retracting his offer to purchase the deed. What she chose to do with it was up to her.

As it should be.

He set down his plume and waited for the ink to dry. Perhaps he would see his landlord once in a while. Or perhaps she would wed sooner than expected and Max would find himself with a new landlord he'd rather not see at all.

It didn't matter. He would stick to the plan. Come morning, he would send the letter and release her from obligation.

No matter how empty the Cloven Hoof felt without her.

He pushed to his feet. His chest ached. It was impossible to keep his mind on business tasks when all he could think about was Bryony. He crossed to the bookshelf on the other side of the room and stared up at a misshapen pillow with astonishingly abysmal craftsmanship.

The corner of his mouth curved. He could not hold Bryony, but he could curl up on the settee and snuggle her handmade pillow to his chest. Perhaps it would even smell of her.

He took it from the shelf and plopped down onto the sofa. If he squinted just right, he could make out the words "Cloven Hoof" and the devil horns embroidered on the linen. He would need to consult the legend to decipher the rest.

This time, he did smile.

Of course she had created a legend. She was hyper-efficient and a worthy opponent in any game. But he had no wish for war. All he wanted was to be her partner. In life. In love.

He lay down on the sofa, legs dangling off the far end, and cuddled the ugly pillow to his chest.

It crinkled.

He frowned and squeezed it to his heart anew.

It crinkled again.

A chuckle escaped his throat. One would think stuffing a pillow with feathers a task even the least artistic hands would be capable of performing. But instead of being soft and comfortable, the pillow was sharp and crunchy instead.

He tried to fluff it.

It crinkled some more.

He turned it over. The backside was not hemmed

shut, as one might suspect, but bisected with a row of buttons. A few stray quill feathers stuck out between the gaps. So did the corner of a piece of parchment.

The pillow case was meant to be opened.

He bolted upright.

In no time, the buttons were undone, the settee littered with feathers, and a stack of parchments trembled in Max's hands.

It wasn't art. It was the deed to his property. Bryony had surrendered it weeks ago. Winning it back from her had never been in question.

He'd had it all along.

Chapter 26

*M*ax stared at the deed in his hands. Was this just like the anonymous donation conscripting Frances to the boarding school? Was this as bad as marrying Bryony to get his hands on her business assets would have been?

Either way, he had wanted to pay for the property, not be handed it out of pity. He wanted it to be true when he said his blood and sweat and tears sacrifice had earned every brick of the Cloven Hoof.

Someone pounded on the door outside.

Not Bryony, of that Max was certain. She had a key. More importantly, she would not be coming back.

He slid the deed beneath a journal on his desk and made his way to the door.

When he swung it open, his sister gazed back at

him. Not in a top hat and lad's clothing, but in a sharp new gown he could only presume had been acquired with her new salary.

He glanced over her shoulder in case she had been spied. "What the devil are you doing here?"

"You stormed off when I told you about my new post teaching dressmaking at a girls' school." She pursed her lips. "I expected something else."

"So did I," he muttered. "You won't take 'charity' from me, but you will from Bryony?"

"Bryony?" Frances repeated in confusion. Her eyes cleared. "The anonymous donation. I had no idea she was involved."

"Very involved," he said bitterly. "She placed you at that school."

"Go to hell," Frances spat, her face twisting in anger. "She didn't place me anywhere."

Max wished he hadn't told her. "The donation—"

"—came with conditions, yes. To hire a teacher with certain capabilities. To offer a given salary. There was no stipulation that I be chosen. Only that the candidate meet expectations." Her voice shook. "I have those capabilities. *I* do. With or without Bryony."

His throat was tight. "Frances—"

"With or without you, either," she added, dark eyes flashing. "I wasn't hired to dump chamber pots.

I met detailed characteristics. I fulfilled the requirements. I successfully passed the vetting process. I submitted to written and oral examination, and interviews with both headmistresses and the children."

His heart clenched. "Fran—"

"I was given an opportunity, not a position. I *earned* the position. To the devil with you for suggesting otherwise." She slammed the door in his face before he could say another word.

He blinked in shock for a few seconds before flinging the door back open and dashing outside in search of his sister.

The only movement was dust flying from the wheels of a hack as it tore off down the street.

Max leaned against the brick façade—a wall that he now owned—and closed his eyes.

Good Lord, had he bollocksed the situation.

From Frances's perspective, there had been no dancing to hidden puppet strings. An opportunity had opened. She could choose to pursue it or not. Of her own volition, she had chosen to pursue it. On her own merit, she had won.

It was not a gift. It was a well-paid responsibility with stringent requirements in both temperament and ability. She met each requirement handily, Max had no doubt.

Frances was right. She had earned this herself. It hadn't been given to her. She had qualified on her own.

A shadow blocked out the sun as Vigo, Max's burly doorman, reported for duty.

"Why are you standing in the alley with the door wide open?" asked the doorman in curiosity.

"Because I'm an imbecile," Max muttered. "It just took me this long to notice."

Vigo laughed. "Don't tell me you are caught up in the 'musicale mystery.'"

Max blinked at him. "Musicale mystery?"

The doorman rolled his eyes. "All the fine gentlemen are positively a-flutter. The Grenvilles have called off all further musicales and no one knows why."

Max furrowed his brow. The Grenville musicales were a London institution. Even after the eldest siblings had married, they continued to perform with the family once or twice a Season. They'd done so for years. A sudden turnabout made no sense.

"What happened?" he asked. Vigo would know. A doorman overheard everything.

"Pawnbroker just came into possession of a Stradivarius in pristine condition." Vigo shook his head in wonder. "One would think a family like the Grenvilles wouldn't need to pawn their most prized possessions for a bit of ready blunt."

Max's lungs tightened.

The heads of the Grenville family did not need to visit pawn shops in order to get their hands on any quantity of coin.

The youngest daughter, however, had no such limitless resources. The purchase of Max's property must have cost Bryony every spare penny she had ever earned.

"A Stradivarius?" he repeated hoarsely. "He is certain?"

Of course the pawnbroker was certain. It was his job to be certain.

"Handed to him by a Grenville chit herself." Vigo made his way toward his post at the front of the club. "Don't be surprised if the end of the Grenville musicales is all anyone speaks of for the next fortnight."

Max's stomach twisted. How badly he had misjudged her. Bryony was not trying to be high-handed and imperious.

The opposite.

She had given up her own future in order to better theirs. Had given him her time, her brain, and her body. Sold her most priceless possession in order to give Frances an opportunity, with no guarantee the gesture would even be accepted.

Bryony had gambled. She had *risked*. She had placed everything she had earned and owned, from her investments to her heart, on the table. And then she had handed her highest trump cards to other players.

She was exactly the woman he had always thought she was. He was the one who had taken a beautiful thing and crumbled it to ash.

Max swung his gaze toward his open office door. At the deed lying upon his desk.

She had given it to him because she wished to. Bryony had not wanted the property to be forced from her. She wished to be able to choose for herself if and when to relinquish it. His heart beat so fast he feared it would burst from his chest. She had handed it over still hoping they might continue to manage the club together, if only from the shadows.

He owed his sister a heartfelt apology, and he owed Bryony so much more.

To continue on without her would be to live in a world without color or music. A dark hole he had finally climbed out of, thanks to her light.

And now she was gone.

Because her parents would forbid their marriage, because Bryony was no longer his landlord, because there was no longer any reason for her to share any part of Max's life.

Unless he gave her one.

He took a deep breath.

The tangles of colored thread upon the pillowcase shone brightly in an office otherwise devoid of color. Everything came to life once Bryony touched it.

With a crooked smile, he remembered her teasing dream of burning down Almack's assembly room and creating a mixed-gender copy of the Cloven Hoof in its place.

His heart skipped. Perhaps the answer had been in front of them all along.

If the Patronesses could run Almack's however they wished, why couldn't he and Bryony run the Cloven Hoof together... and open it to everyone? Why couldn't they both win?

There would be outcry, of course. Just like when the club first opened and a few high-in-the-instep lords publicly protested the Cloven Hoof for allowing entry to people they felt beneath them.

Women were not beneath men. Frances proved it. Bryony proved it. Her sisters proved it. Any gentleman who couldn't handle the idea of men and women sharing a common space for gaming and good conversation could just keep walking.

Of course, such a fanciful idea hinged on Bryony wishing to have anything to do with Max at all.

He would not force her to associate with him. But he would do as she had done for Frances, and give her an opportunity. One she could choose to take or to leave. One she had earned.

He strode from the Cloven Hoof and hailed the first passing hack. There were two stops to make before heading to Bryony's house and handing her the keys to her own future. Before she had given him the deed to the Cloven Hoof, he already owned the empty storefront next door.

Not for long.

She would soon be in possession of the deed.

It meant giving up on his dreams for the Cloven Hoof. For her.

He didn't expect accolades. It didn't even mean she would forgive him. He wanted to do the right thing. To surrender the possession *he* most cared about in all the world.

What Bryony would do with the property, he had no idea. She was certainly clever enough to establish an even better club and put him out of business. Or she could sell the deed to anyone but him if all she wanted was to purchase her Stradivarius back.

There was no way to know. It didn't matter. Her life and her choices were up to her. As they should be.

Within the space of an hour, Max presented himself at the home of Lord and Lady Grenville.

A place he'd sworn he'd never go.

A place he knew he was not welcome.

He might well be turned away at the door. Thrown into the street like so much rubbish.

It didn't matter.

All that mattered was Bryony. He would beg forgiveness from her, and her hand from her father.

No matter the odds, he needed to try.

He banged the gilt knocker.

An impassive butler answered the door. "Calling card?"

Damn it. Max stared back at him in consternation.

"Who is it, Prate?" came Bryony's voice from just around the corner.

"Maxwell Gideon, here to deliver an apology," Max announced in a voice loud enough to carry.

Silence reigned.

He would not yet tell her about the property next door to the Cloven Hoof. It was irrelevant.

She would get the deed whether she forgave him or not.

He needed her to know he loved her without conditions or expectations. Exactly who and how she was.

That was, if she allowed him to cross this threshold.

Chapter 27

*B*ryony's fingers tightened on her book in disbelief.

She was alone in the family drawing room, an untouched pile of samplers at her side. Instead of embroidering, she was engrossed in *The Castle of Otranto* by Horace Walpole. She had filched the volume from Max's office.

And now he was here. Why? What else could be left to say?

Bryony set the book aside and pushed to her feet. It would be churlish to refuse an apology. Her heart thumped. Nor was there any sense in avoiding him. Not when he already filled her every thought.

She walked toward the door and stopped short behind her butler. "Why are you here?"

Max cleared his throat. "May I come in?"

She crossed her arms. "No."

"Very well." He took a deep breath. "I'm in love with you, Bryony Grenville. I know I am not what your parents hoped. I'm not even what you had hoped. But I love you. I wanted you to know."

Her heart cracked a little. "Anything else?"

"I didn't mean to hurt you." His words were filled with self-loathing. "I was the one who didn't think before acting. You didn't deserve that. I'm sorry."

Her heart fluttered. They had both been rash. They had both been wrong. What mattered was that they were able to discuss their feelings. To forgive. To help each other be better.

"Is that all?" she asked, her voice softer this time.

"It is not all." With a flourish, he thrust a kitten-sized blob of blindingly red fabric in her direction. "This is for you."

Curiosity won out.

She uncrossed her arms and stepped forward to accept what deductive reasoning would have her believe was a cushion of some kind. An uncomfortable one. What with sharp quill ends sticking out through the fabric at every angle.

"Impressive," she said. "You managed to make it worse than mine."

"It's heart-shaped," he said helpfully.

She gave it a few skeptical turns. "Is it?"

He dropped to one knee in supplication. "I am forced to present you with a poor facsimile because you already possess the real thing. You are the keeper of my heart and the greatest partner a man could ever hope to find. I would like to be yours forever. Would you do me the honor of being my bride?"

Bryony's eyes shone with tears. There was nothing she wanted more.

But before she could respond, the soft footfalls of her mother's slippers hurried down the stairs.

"What is this?" Mother demanded shrilly. "Was I not clear?"

"You were cruel," Bryony corrected, not bothering to hide the anger in her voice. "You publicly humiliated the man that I love for no reason at all."

"You love me?" Max's grin lit his eyes. "You *love* me."

"Of course I love you." Bryony set her fists on her hips in exasperation. "What other conclusion could be drawn from more than a month's worth of behavioral observation?"

"I told you not to talk like that," Mother interrupted fretfully. "People will hear you."

Bryony did not respond. All her attention was focused on the long-haired rogue on one knee before her.

She knelt to join him.

"Yes." She took his hands. "I will marry you. I've analyzed my calculations several times and come to the only conclusion that matters. Living together creates increased opportunities for biscuit-making. And biscuits lead to—"

"Absolutely not," Mother grabbed Bryony's elbow and yanked her to her side. "I forbid it."

Max leaped to his feet. "Lady Grenville—"

"You will not address me," Mother interrupted without even looking his way. Her eyes were on Bryony. "And you will not either if you continue down this path. I will lock you away if I have to."

Bryony wrenched her arm from her mother's grip and reached out toward Max. "Do you have any plans for tonight? How much is a hack to Gretna Green?"

He stared at her in stunned silence then pulled her into his protective embrace. "The same plans I have every night for the rest of my life. Making you happy, anyway that I can."

Mother's face was bright purple. "You would choose him even knowing it means being cut off from your parents and every shilling we have?"

Bryony didn't let go of his hand. "I choose Max *especially* if that's what it means. I love him. That's all that matters. He is worth more than all the shillings in the world."

Max stiffened. "I didn't mean for you to lose your family."

"Think carefully!" Mother's voice was shrill and panicked. "I just want what is best for my child and her future. This is your last chance to make the right choice."

"I have done so," Bryony replied evenly. "If my happiness with Max means cutting ties with you, that is a decision you have made without me."

Mother's lower lip trembled. "You would choose exile over your own family?"

"The other side of London isn't *exile*," Bryony pointed out dryly. "And Max *is* family. He is not the one forcing me to choose. You are."

"I don't want you to choose him," Mother stammered, in obvious shock that even the threat of banishment did not aid her cause. "You are a Grenville."

"Not for long." Bryony lifted Max's pillow. "He's given me his heart. I've already given him mine."

To make the point, she hugged the pillow to her chest.

It crinkled.

She whirled toward Max in surprise and accusation. "You found the deed!"

"I found the deed," he agreed.

Her pulse raced in frustration. "I didn't give it to you just for you to give it right back to me!"

"I'm not that much of a gentleman," he promised. "Open it."

She ripped open the pillow and pulled out a folded square of parchment.

It *was* a deed, but not to the Cloven Hoof. This certificate granted ownership of the property next door.

She stared up at him. "You bought this for me?"

"I bought it for me," he admitted. "Before I met you. But once I heard the sound business reasons behind your plot to set fire to Almack's—"

"*What?*" Mother choked out in horror. "Now listen to me, Bryony Prudence Grenville. I really will cut you off if you—"

Bryony gazed up at Max. "Instead of expanding the Cloven Hoof, you're letting me create a competing club?"

"If that's what you want to do." His dark eyes were intent on hers. "Alternatively, we can create complementary clubs. Or expand the Cloven Hoof together, using your ideas about diversity not just in class, but inclusivity of gender. No matter what you do with that deed, all my future decisions will be choices made *with* you. We're a team."

Bryony threw her arms about his neck and held him so tight she trembled.

This was why he was the perfect man for her. He saw her as an equal. He didn't just value her ideas and independence. He valued *her*. He valued the two of them, together.

"We'll be unstoppable," she said when she'd finally regained her composure. "We'll revolutionize entertainment clubs. Create a new standard of our own design. We'll make more money than we will know what to do with."

"I hear your sister has some sort of charity," he

offered, with a crooked smile.

Bryony grinned at him. "Let's take London by storm."

"You... don't care about your dowry?" Mother stammered in dawning realization.

"I have never cared about my dowry," Bryony answered, "or wished for a man who did. You and Father are important to me because you're my parents, not because I'm after your purse strings."

Heavy footsteps sounded upon the stair.

Bryony's heart sank.

"What's this uproar?" called Bryony's father in irritation. "Can't a man have any peace and quiet in his own home?"

Mother positioned herself between her husband and her daughter, her gaze focused tight on Bryony. "We *are* important to you?"

"You're family," Bryony said simply. "I'm simply trying to add to it. You were the one who threatened to cut me off for following my heart."

Mother swallowed. "I wanted you to do as I asked, not agree to be cut off. The house will be empty enough without you in it. I never wished to lose you from my life completely."

"What's happening?" Father demanded impatiently. He narrowed his eyes at Max. "Why is he here?"

"To ask for your daughter's hand," Max said, his voice polite and calm.

Father's brow creased in confusion. "My Bryony? Wed the Lord of Vice?"

Bryony tightened her hold on Max's hand. "I love him. With or without your blessing, we—"

"They'll run off to Gretna Green and we'll never see them again," Mother interrupted in a burst, the words tripping over each other. "He doesn't want the dowry. He wants our daughter, and she wants him."

Father stared at her in disbelief. "Are you saying you agree to the match?"

Bryony held her breath, her heart beating triple-time.

"I'm saying she's our daughter," Mother said at last. "Family doesn't turn its back on family."

"Would you come to the wedding?" Bryony asked, not daring to hope. "If Max and I didn't elope?"

Mother turned toward the baron. "If your father gives permission."

In that moment, Bryony realized her mother was asking on behalf of all of them. Permission for Max to ask for Bryony's hand, permission for Bryony to accept, permission for herself as both a mother and a baroness to support the match and be happy for her child. Permission to be present at her daughter's wedding.

"Very well," Father said, with a glance at his pocketwatch. "I'll summon you after the contracts have been drawn up."

He immediately turned and headed back upstairs toward his study.

Bryony wasn't hurt at the abrupt dismissal. She was shocked that her father had spared this much time for her at all, and over the moon that the answer had been yes.

She leaned against Max's powerful frame. "Do you mind a traditional wedding?"

"My sister would kill me if I robbed her of the opportunity to design the perfect trousseau for both of us," he admitted. "A few weeks of banns should be just enough time."

Mother's eyes shone with interest. "Your sister is a modiste? Dreadful that she should be in trade, but I do love being the first to know about these things. Is she particularly gifted?"

"Only the most talented seamstress in all of London," Bryony replied, knowing full well her mother was unable to resist portraying herself as the height of fashion. With a reputation like that, Mother would be dying for an introduction, even if her pride would not yet allow her to admit it.

Bryony grinned to herself. Perhaps in the future, the Cloven Hoof would not be the only locale to feature gatherings of a diverse range of classes and gender and backgrounds.

Perhaps going forward, inclusivity could even start at home.

Chapter 28

Two weeks later
The day the first banns are read

𝒩 ow that the Season was no longer in full swing and no more musicales were on the horizon, Bryony's mother had turned her attentions to starting a new family tradition. Annual gatherings featuring one dinner, both parents, and all of the siblings.

Bryony wasn't certain which was the greater achievement: that Mother had indeed managed to coax Father down from his office to the dinner table, or that every member of her extended family was present, Grenvilles and honorary Grenvilles alike.

Heath, Simon, and Lord Wainwright were at the refreshment table, valiantly attempting to choke down Bryony's latest batch of marginally more edible biscuits.

Frances and Bryony's mother were side-by-side on the sofa, heads bent over fashion plates as they planned everyone's wardrobes for the upcoming wedding.

Dahlia, along with her co-headmistress Faith and her family, were jostling amid a tornado of fluttering playing-cards.

Heath's wife Nora sat in the corner with a sketchbook, capturing the entirety of the scene with her pencil. A small pug slept in a basket at her feet.

Bryony slipped her fingers into Max's hand for a quick squeeze. "What'll it be? Fashion plates or the refreshment table?"

"Brandy?" Max asked hopefully.

She snorted. "You don't imbibe."

"This seems a logical time to start," he muttered. "Your father is heading this way."

Bryony straightened her spine.

Father had finished his obligatory post-supper glass of port and was clearly on his way to the stairs leading back up to his office. But first, he paused briefly in front of Bryony and Max.

With his empty wineglass, he gestured toward a box in the corner. "Wedding gift."

"For us?" Bryony stammered. She wasn't certain her father had ever noticed her long enough to gift her anything before.

"For your mother," he said with a shake of his

head. "Perhaps now she'll cease complaining."

With that, he continued on up the stairs.

Bryony exchanged baffled glances with Max.

"Open it," he whispered. "Maybe it contains someone who knows how to make better biscuits."

She elbowed him in the ribs.

Together, they walked over to the box and lifted the lid. Bryony gasped in wonder.

Inside was a new Stradivarius.

"Music is an excellent gift." Max's gaze softened. "I might come to like your father after all."

Bryony ran her finger down along the delicate curves of the violin's body. "It's beautiful."

"You are beautiful." Max stepped away from the instrument. "Do you want to play it?"

She did, actually. It had been so long since she'd created music. She plucked lightly at the strings and grinned at the realization that the instrument was in tune. Perfect in every way. Practically begging for her touch.

Now that the musicales had been canceled, she could play because she *wished* to. Not out of duty, but because she loved music.

As soon as her bow touched the strings, her family and friends leapt to their feet and came together in a lively country-dance.

Everyone except Max. He had eyes only for her.

When the song came to an end, she reverently placed the Stradivarius back into its case. It was like the final piece had been returned to her heart.

"No more music?" asked the Hawkridge's ward, Christina.

Heath immediately seated himself at the pianoforte. "A waltz, in honor of the upcoming bride and groom!"

Max glanced down at her in question.

She placed her hand in his. "Waltz with me, my lord."

"I'm no lord," he growled.

"That's what I like best about you," she said with a wicked smile. "That, and your forked tail."

He whirled her into his arms, likely to stop her from talking.

Bryony didn't mind. All she cared about was staying in Max's embrace, now and forever.

His eyes hooded. "Do you have plans after the wedding?"

She gave him a saucy grin. "Do I ever. Unfortunately, the wedding breakfast comes first. Unless you have something else in mind?"

"A grand opening." His eyes glittered. "It seems only fitting that the Cloven Hoof's sister club should share our anniversary. After all, we are building it together."

A thrill ran through her. *Their grand opening.*

At last.

"Is anyone watching us?" she whispered.

He glanced over her shoulder. "No one."

She pulled him out of the drawing room and into the shadows, where nothing could keep her lips from finding his.

Epilogue

Four months later

*M*ax darted across freshly-swept cobble-stones to admire a view of the twin clubs from across the street. It had been three weeks since the grand opening and he still couldn't get enough.

On the left was the Cloven Hoof. Austere, dark, mysterious. Dedicated wholly to gambling. As always, the windows were darkened so as to block out both sunlight and the curious gazes of passersby. Unlike before, the games inside were now open to both men and women.

Standing beside the closed door with his thick arms folded over his barrel chest was Vigo. He was lost in conversation. Talking animatedly at his side stood a French poet in champagne-shined Hessians, a spangled waistcoat, and a pair of gold rimmed spectacles.

There was plenty of time for them to talk. The doors wouldn't open for another hour.

The façade to the right boasted large glass windows, welcoming in both the light and anyone who chanced to pass by, man or woman. Bryony perched on a stool by the door, Vigo's unlikely counterpart in a satin evening gown and scuffed top hat.

Her sister-in-law had not only designed the signage for the new addition, but painted the door herself. *THE CROOKED HALO*, declared the bold text, curving above a winged cherub with a wicked grin, a pair of almost imperceptible horns, and yes, a crooked halo. It was perfect.

Max's life couldn't be happier. His wife was stupendous. Together, they accomplished more than either possibly could alone.

In the weeks since the Crooked Halo's grand opening, they had already seen positive impact. The front salon was primarily used as conversation nooks where poets, intellectuals, book clubs, and the like could gather for an exchange of ideas and opinions.

The public's response had been tremendous. Especially after a certain caricature had made the rounds, featuring the Cloven Hoof's infamous Lord of Vice reading love sonnets to his wife in front of their peers. Everyone had come to see.

Last week, Bryony had set up a small stage to be used at the twilight hour, by those who wished to share music, poetry, or other art with fellow patrons. Max was still shocked at the number and variety of talented people who flocked to the salon to see and be seen.

The rear chamber of the new annex was reserved for individuals who preferred not to gamble real money. Bryony had stocked the room with an overabundance of playing-cards, and overnight the Grenville family game had become household knowledge. It was now known as "playing Crooked Halo."

They had even installed a swinging door between the Cloven Hoof and the Crooked Halo, for patrons who wished to wander back and forth between them.

This had proven to be a stroke of brilliance, increasing profits and curiosity on both sides. The passageway allowed for more opportunities to please mixed crowds, in which some guests fancied a game of loo whilst others in their party preferred to debate the merits of iambic pentameter or Gothic symbolism.

Or the joy of tossing a handful of playing cards in each other's faces.

Their joint establishments had something for everyone.

Before the evening's inevitable crowd descended upon them, Max crossed the street and swung his wife up into his arms.

"Careful," she teased. "You'll dislodge my halo."

"I'm the devil of the Cloven Hoof," he murmured into her neck. "I do as I please."

She arched a brow. "And what, might a lady ask, would please a devil like you?"

"*You*," he growled and gave her a kiss that could be felt all the way to the heavens.

Acknowledgments

As always, I could not have written this book without the invaluable support of my critique partners. Huge thanks go out to Erica Monroe and Emma Locke. You are the best!

Lastly, I want to thank the *Rogues to Riches* facebook group, my *Historical Romance Book Club*, and my fabulous street team. Your enthusiasm makes the romance happen.

Thank you so much!

Thank You for Reading

I hope you enjoyed this story!

Sign up at http://ridley.vip
for members-only freebies
and special deals for 99 cents!

Did you know there are more books in this series?

This romance is part of
the *Rogues to Riches*
regency-set historical series.

In order, the *Rogues to Riches* books are:

Lord of Chance
Lord of Pleasure
Lord of Night
Lord of Temptation
Lord of Secrets
Lord of Vice

Join the *Rogues to Riches* Facebook group for giveaways
and exclusive content:
http://facebook.com/groups/RoguesToRiches

In order, the *Dukes of War* books are:

The Viscount's Christmas Temptation
The Earl's Defiant Wallflower
The Captain's Bluestocking Mistress
The Major's Faux Fiancée
The Brigadier's Runaway Bride
The Pirate's Tempting Stowaway
The Duke's Accidental Wife

Join the *Dukes of War* Facebook group for giveaways
and exclusive content:
http://facebook.com/groups/DukesOfWar

About the Author

Erica Ridley is a *New York Times* and *USA Today* bestselling author of historical romance novels.

In the new *Rogues to Riches* historical romance series, Cinderella stories aren't just for princesses… Sighworthy Regency rogues sweep strong-willed young ladies into whirlwind rags-to-riches romance with rollicking adventure.

The popular *Dukes of War* series features roguish peers and dashing war heroes who return from battle only to be thrust into the splendor and madness of Regency England.

When not reading or writing romances, Erica can be found riding camels in Africa, zip-lining through rainforests in Central America, or getting hopelessly lost in the middle of Budapest.

For more information, visit www.EricaRidley.com.

CPSIA information can be obtained
at www.ICGtesting.com
Printed in the USA
LVHW092242080321
680948LV00024B/348